CORRODED CELLS

A CYBERPUNK SAGA

MATTHEW A. GOODWIN

CORRODED CELLS

A Cyberpunk Saga
Book 2
MATTHEW A. GOODWIN

Independently published via KDP

ISBN Number 978-1-7340692-9-7

Editor: Bookhelpline.com

Cover design by Coversbychristian.com

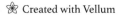 Created with Vellum

For my parents, who always supported my creative endeavors and my brother, who played makeshift D&D with me when no one else would.

PART I

CHAPTER 1

M oss stood on the roof of an aging apartment building, the heavy fog glowing from the street signs below. It was time. Any moment now the convoy would pass just overhead. He stood in waiting—a snake ready to strike. Patchwork had hacked the log and had the schedule down to the second. This run was for him. He needed new hardware for his computers, and while it was very expensive on the black market, it was free to steal from D2E—the entertainment conglomerate who ran the world's television and internet.

"You ready?" Moss asked of his friend Gibbs, laying on the roof next to him. He had a long rifle in his hands and was looking through the auto-scoping lens.

"You knowdely know it, Neddy," he said in an impression of some long-forgotten television show or movie which Moss didn't recognize. Gibbs had been learning to shoot and was getting better. After the big raid against ThutoCo, Gibbs had felt useless and demanded someone teach him a skill. He had enjoyed seeing the world from above and calling out what he saw, so shooting from afar seemed to be a good fit.

They are approaching, Patchwork, their resident breaker and all-around computer whiz said in their minds on their secure network.

Moss turned on his dronepack and began hovering off the roof. No automated coordinates now—he controlled the movement with his neural implant. Patchwork had unlocked further functionality when he hacked the implant to ensure ThutoCo couldn't get to him. After they blew up part of the headquarter building, destroying their technology and exposing the evil plan, they had been taking every measure to prepare for retaliation from the megacorporation. None had come yet. Moss lifted his launcher and readied himself as the convoy passed overhead. He fired, feeling the recoil as the arachnotensil cable rocketed forward and magnetized to the side of the transport, and pulled against where the other side had been attached to the roof.

Moss saw Ynna's cable fly nearly simultaneously and the two tows stopped the transport dead in the air as the guard cars zipped forward before the programs realized what happened. The transport boosted its thrusters, pulling hard against the anchored cords. Moss and Ynna flew up next to the struggling vehicle as the escorts turned back.

Gibbs fired a massive, explosive bullet through the engine of one, sending it careening toward the street below, a trail of smoke in its wake. Two passed through the smoke, their targeting disrupted by the plumes. One dropped a mounted machine gun from its base and opened fire on Gibbs—or so it thought. He had set up a small projector to the rear to produce a heated image of himself elsewhere on the roof. Bullets passed through the projection, shredding the tar and drywall down to the rebar.

Gibbs shot back, the heavy weapon thudding against its

bipod, the metal legs sinking into the tar. The bullet whistled through the air, striking the flighted car's energy converter, causing the machine to sputter and plummet directly down.

The other two spun back on Gibbs as Ynna and Moss mounted the transport, using heavy lasers to cut the doors open. They had to wear heavy masks and goggles, making it hard to see and maneuver while floating above the city street. There was commotion below, the two downed vehicles stopping traffic and attracting onlookers. People were pointing up, filming with their devices.

"Time's running out," Ynna said as she yanked one of the doors open and clambered inside. Ynna was a smart and capable street samurai who had been running with this crew for a long time. Moss knew if she said they were short on time, they were.

He dropped his slicer, gloves, and goggles to the ground, the massive weapon landing with a crash atop one of the cars far below. He darted around to the other side and joined Ynna inside as they heard Gibbs take down one more guard car.

"He's getting good," Moss observed. Ynna smiled.

"Getting there," she said, looking around and trying to find the specific motherboard Patchwork had told them to look for. "He wastes too much time trying to get us all to watch old movies and shit. Time he could be spending honing a craft."

"Cut him some slack," Moss said absently, his eyes darting around, trying to find the hardware. "This is the most focused I've seen him get on anything."

"Liar," Ynna laughed, and Moss paused, turning to look at her while the vehicle shook and pulled, the autopilot still trying to break free.

Moss stopped a moment to look at her with confusion. "What?"

"If he had spent half as much energy applying himself to

anything as he did playing video games and chasing tail, he could be an expert marksman," Ynna said, holding the rattling cage of supplies inside the vehicle for support. The space was tight and filled with computer equipment. Patchwork had told them what they were looking for, but it was hard to know exactly.

"You seeing anything?" Moss asked.

"Not really," Ynna said. "All looks the same to me."

The vehicle shook violently as one of the escorts passed close overhead, the sound of shells falling on the roof like a brief rain. They both kept looking hurriedly, knowing Carcer Corp would already be on their way. This crew had massive bounties on them, and they could not get caught over something like this. Moss pulled open cabinets, still not finding what they were looking for.

"It's got a diamond," Ynna began helpfully.

"Diamond in the middle with two red stripes," Moss filled in. "I remember, he said it a thousand times."

An explosion rocked the vehicle, sending it lurching down before the thrusters activated once more.

"We really have to hurry," Ynna said, more to herself than to Moss.

"I know it," Moss agreed.

What's taking you guys? Patchwork asked from the comfort of the safe house, transmitting through a neural network.

"Looking as fast as we can." Moss couldn't help himself from answering aloud.

It's got a diamond, Patchwork began.

"Diamond in the middle with two red stripes," Moss and Ynna said together. The car rattled and exploded as the remaining escort let forth a barrage on the side of the vehicle.

"Human control, we have to fucking hurry!" Ynna ordered, knowing the program would never fire its weapons at a car it was escorting. Moss was now throwing things aside, moving through piles of machinery as he looked. Perspiration built on his forehead. It wasn't supposed to take this long.

Carcer en route. I intercepted and sent them the wrong way, but it won't be long 'till they figure it out, Patchwork informed them. His frayed nerves were clear even through the thought message.

"Shit!" Moss said, shoving some panels out of the way and hearing a loose clink. He looked and saw that there was a false panel behind the equipment. He pried, shoving his fingers behind the panel and pulling hard. It popped loose and revealed the motherboard they were looking for. "Gotcha," he beamed. Ynna rushed over so Patchwork could look through her augmented eyes.

That's it! He told them. Now get out of there. Moss wrapped the motherboard in some loose cloth and placed it delicately in a satchel. They knew one of the guard cars was still circling them.

"Release cables on my three," Ynna ordered as she leaped from the door. "One, two," and Moss jumped out too, ordering his cable to demagnetize. The car lurched forward as he blasted out into the air, the guard car hit on its heels. The human operator shot wide of Moss and Ynna, peppering a nearby building with machine gun fire, spraying chunks of bricks and dust into the air.

Drones moving in, Patchwork told them. *Only two though*, he amended. Moss pulled his Kingfisher electron pistol from its holster and waited for the buzz. It only took a moment, but with the sounds of their propellers came an announcement.

"ThutoCo employee number 06187300, the Carcer Corporation has a message regar—" it began before Ynna blasted one out of the sky while Gibbs destroyed the other.

"Wait," Moss yelled, but it was too late, the two drones already littered the street below. Gibbs joined them in the air as the final escort circled back on them for one more pass. They shimmered into projected cloaks and became invisible to the machine gunner sitting at a computer somewhere.

They flew back to the safe house, Moss wondering the whole time what message Carcer had and why it was for him. They landed and packed up, bringing the new gear to Patchwork.

"Yessss," he said excitedly, grinning from ear to ear. "You guys are my heroes."

"What was that?" Gibbs asked Moss. "That was your number, right?"

"It was, and now I want to know," Moss answered, pulling his gear from his body.

Ynna looked at them gravely. "I'm sure it was a trap, whatever it was."

"No doubt," Moss agreed, but the broken message piqued his curiosity. He did not know why Carcer had singled him out, but he wanted to know.

"You still want to know, don't you?" Ynna rolled her eyes and chucked her gloves quickly at him.

He caught one as the other thudded against his chest and fell to the ground. "I really do," Moss admitted.

"Let me ask you this," Gibbs began in a serious tone, picking up the glove and handing it back to Ynna.

"I swear, if you suggest a pros and cons list," Ynna said, shaking a fist in mock threat.

"I wasn't," he said defensively. "I was going to ask what they could possibly have that we, or more accurately, Moss wants."

"I don't know," Moss answered. "Issy and her dad are too far underground to be unearthed, and the rest of the crew are just out getting lunch, right?"

"Yeah, I have a fix on their beacons. They're fine," Patchwork said.

"You don't think?" Gibbs said suggestively, covering one eye with his hand.

"No," Ynna announced. "Burn was one foot in the grave when we left him, and he would never have let himself be taken alive."

"Sorry," Gibbs said. "I was just speaking out loud."

"What? As opposed to speaking silently? You mean you were thinking out loud," she admonished in a tone which was only half-joking. Moss was growing impatient. He knew how she liked to get Gibbs all flummoxed, but now was not the time.

"Patch, can you get me a line so secure I could receive a message without Carcer tracing it?" Moss asked. Patchwork stroked his chin in theatrical consideration.

"Not for long, honestly," he mumbled. He never liked to admit his own limitations. "If they sent a message for the express purpose of catching you, they will have an army of breakers trying to get a fix on us, and I couldn't stop them all."

"Damn," Moss said. "What about the Church?"

"You've used those servers before, and they will have traced it by now. You probably couldn't walk within a thousand meters of that place without being picked up," Patchwork explained. "Now, I mean, if you are dead set on doing this," he let the moment hang.

"I am," Moss said. He had been testing the water at first, but now he wanted to know what Carcer had on him.

"There are places," Patchwork said. "Breaker's dens where we could get you a clean line. But they are dangerous and expensive."

"Money, we've got," Ynna said, and it was true. Since they had exposed ThutoCo, many parties had been funneling money to the crews, helping to fund the cause of freedom from the large companies. Many were family members of people who were employees under unbreakable contracts or friends of people jailed in Carcer City.

Seti, the eye in the sky for all the groups working to fight the companies, somehow rinsed the electronic currency clean and got it out. They were flush. They had bought new weapons and clothes, set up more safe houses and, at Gibbs request, cleaned the one they were currently living in.

"It's not money they want," Patchwork said with a hangdog expression. Moss looked down, patted the satchel and glanced up to see him nodding.

"At least it won't go to waste," Moss offered.

"It might if it's nothing more than a trap," Gibbs noted.

"Not helping," Moss snapped as the door from the stairwell opened and Judy and Stan entered. The massive man looked so different now to Moss. He had lost his arm in the ThutoCo attack and was unwilling to have a replacement put on.

So many people augmented their bodies for vanity reasons or to compete with drudges for jobs, but Stan wanted to remain all human and would not allow it. He was determined not to let it hinder him despite Judy, his lover's, protestations.

Unlike Stan, Judy had gone through many surgeries and augmentations in their life to become genderless. They worked as the group's fixer and made no secret of their desire to see Stan patched. Though Judy loved the man, they had no qualm in telling him how they felt about his choice.

"What's doing here?" Stan asked in his slight drawl.

"Moss wants to get a message from Carcer," Ynna informed them.

"It's a trap," Judy and Stan said in unison, and Gibbs chuckled to himself.

"He knows, but you know how he gets," Ynna said, and the two nodded.

"Let it go, man," Stan warned him. "Nothing good will come of engaging with them."

"But—" Moss began.

"But nothing. Seriously, let it drop," he said, his voice growing low and severe. He turned to Ynna. "How did the mission go?"

"Good, we got the new toy," she said.

"It's not a toy, and Moss wants to trade it," Patchwork said like a disappointed child.

"Just give me the day to think about it," Moss offered.

"Fine," Patchwork said and turned back to his bank of monitors to sulk, feeling even more foolish for suggesting it could be traded away.

"Where are Grimy and CT?" Ynna asked.

"Grimy said he'd be right back and CT is at a club, undoubtedly getting shot down by women out of his league," Stan said with a grin.

"Oh, and he didn't bring Gibbs?" Ynna laughed and turned to him. "Getting shot down by girls is kind of a specialty of yours, isn't it?"

"My charms aren't lost on everyone," Gibbs defended, but Moss could tell he was hurt.

"It's true," Moss put in. "He ever tell you guys about the Butler twins?"

"Twins?" Ynna guffawed, but Gibbs lit up.

"Yes!" Gibbs said and regaled them with a tale, leaving out the part that it was robotic counterparts rather than the real thing.

They all looked relieved as Grimy strode in, a hat box under one arm. The former veterinarian turned street medic loved his finery and could talk ad nauseam about suits and hats the way Gibbs could about girls.

"You hit my old stomping grounds?" Ynna asked.

Grimy smiled as he set his box down and began pulling one of his white gloves off one finger at a time. "I did. Redwood Point may be the slum of slums, but Maurice still makes the best hats in the city."

Ynna rolled her eyes. "Man, Grimy, I still can't believe it was *you* who brought me into this life," she said. Ynna had told Moss the story of how she was lying beaten and bloody on the streets when Grimy scared off the thugs and brought her into the crew.

"Don't you forget it," he said with a wink and made his way to the bathroom.

As he did, the door opened, and Chicken Thumbs walked in.

Gibbs hooted. "It's like TV timing in here."

Ynna gave him a sideways glance as everyone in the room pretended to ignore Stan and Judy making out and groping each other on a cot.

"Yeah," Gibbs said, pointing to CT. "One character exits just as the other enters."

"I'm not a character," CT whined but everyone ignored him.

"That's actually pretty clever," Ynna told Gibbs, giving a little wink. Moss watched as the corner of his friend's lip turned up slightly.

Ynna turned to Chicken Thumbs and gave him a playful shove. "Stan said you were off getting laid."

CT flushed. "Laying the groundwork."

"Aww," Ynna mocked sympathy. "And what you really wanted to do was lay some pipe."

"Fuck off, Ynna," CT snorted and made his way to the fridge for a beer.

"Love you, too," Ynna said and threw the hatbox at him, striking him on the back before falling to the floor.

From inside the bathroom, Grimy called out, "I heard that."

Moss smiled, happy to see his friends happy after a successful mission.

. . .

IN THE DEAD OF NIGHT, he was awakened by a tap on the shoulder and a sweaty palm over his mouth. His eyes went wide with terror until he saw his friend's face. Gibbs was illuminated by the blue light of the power indicators of all the electronics around the room.

"Let's do it," he whispered softly, holding up the satchel.

CHAPTER 2

Moss slid out of bed. He slept in his clothes so he simply needed to grab his gun and trench coat so they could leave. He pulled his black coat over the black shirt with black jeans which made up his look and smiled. He was happy Gibbs had done this. His night had been fitful, spent tossing and turning, his mind unable to let go. He got geared up as quietly as he could, the sound covered by Stan snoring. They easily navigated the space in the low light and exited into the stairwell, closing the door behind them. They were startled as they turned, Judy looking up at them with high, glassy eyes.

"I won't tell," Judy said too loudly for Moss's taste, nursing a glass of pruno.

"Thanks," Gibbs whispered.

"Fucking stupid though," Judy told them.

"Maybe," Moss had to admit. He knew this could be a mistake, a trap, but he couldn't shake the feeling that there was something he needed to know.

"Don't get killed, they're starting to like you," Judy said, head rolling with the words.

"Yeah," Gibbs said with a slight smile. "You all right?"

Judy snorted, "Just fucking dandy."

"See you in the morning, Judy," Moss said as they began to walk down the stairs.

"Afternoon, more like," Gibbs whispered.

Moss nodded. "Yeah."

THE STREET WAS as alive at night as during the day, but with a different type of people. The safe house was in an apartment complex near the rail station, and in the light of day, people bustled about, heading to work. At night, the streets were abuzz with the people who slept all day—hoods pulled up to shield their eyes from the neon street signs. Off to the right, folks danced in the street to the sound of an impromptu concert on apartment steps. Vendors pushed carts with food being sold on top and other, more nefarious items for sale hidden away.

They pushed through the people, Moss turning to ask, "You know where we are going?"

"Yeah," Gibbs said, leading the way. "I ask a lot of questions anyway, so Patch wasn't suspicious when I got the lowdown."

"Thank goodness for your curious nature," Moss said and clapped his friend on the shoulder. "Thank you for doing this."

"What are friends for, right?" Gibbs said with a smile. "Shall we?" He pointed to a street vendor making quesadillas on an open skillet.

"Let's," Moss said, and they ordered.

"Can you believe how we used to eat?" Gibbs asked, mouth full, cheese dripping down his chin.

"Seemed good at the time," Moss said. "Didn't know any better."

"We were so dumb," Gibbs observed as they walked to the rail station.

"Right, the food is the thing we were naïve about," Moss said sarcastically.

"Among many things," Gibbs amended. "You hear ThutoCo may go belly up? People are sneaking out, breaking their contracts, fleeing to the city from the Burbs."

"I have. I hope it's true," Moss said.

"We did that," Gibbs bragged.

"We did," Moss said with cautious pride. "But ThutoCo will survive."

"I'm sure you're right, much as it pains me," Gibbs admitted. "You talk to Issy?"

"Almost every day," Moss said. They had helped their oldest friend escape from the grips of ThutoCo, and now she was in hiding with her father in the Old Oak district of the city. "Vihaan started a small restaurant she is helping to run."

"That's great," Gibbs said. "You wish she had stayed with us?"

"For myself, yes. Having you guys around makes this whole thing easier, but I know it's what she needs, so I'm happy for her."

"That's it?" Gibbs pressed.

"That's all I have the bandwidth for," Moss said, not wanting to admit how much it pained him that they were apart. "What's up with you and Ynna?"

"What?" he answered all too defensively. "I mean, she's hot, but she's a first-rate ball buster, and I'm pretty sure I'm not her type anyway."

"You sure about that?" Moss asked despite the unease of his friend. Gibbs tended toward bravado and bluster over feelings and introspection.

"She wants a guy who kicks in doors and fucks up bad guys," Gibbs said. Moss laughed.

"She is those things. I'm not sure she's looking for herself in a partner," he explained.

Gibbs snorted. "Agree to disagree."

"As ever," Moss said as they boarded the railcar. It was a long tube with plastic chairs and metal handrails with windows along the walls and ad screens covering the ceilings. Everyone moved to find seats, trying to avoid the vomit and garbage which littered the ground, before returning to their palmscreens or lenscreens. No one spoke; everyone simply retreated into their digital worlds as the railcar carried their physical forms along. A filthy man pushed through, trying to snag people's attention long enough to ask for a money transfer. He approached them, his layers of clothes smelling of urine.

"Help me out? I served," he asked, the words hoarse, his voice quiet with disuse. He held up an aged palmscreen displaying an account number, and Gibbs answered.

"I got you," he used his neural implant to transfer five bucks.

"Thank you, brother," he said, a brief glint in his hollow eyes. He shuffled away, ignored by everyone.

"It doesn't help," Moss said, looking on the man with pity.

"Maybe, maybe not. But I'm happy to bring any light into this dark world," he said in the oppressive brightness of the overhead screens. Moss smiled at the notion. They had been through so much since leaving the Burbs—seen so much—but Gibbs had not lost his spirit. Moss admired him, wanted what his friend seemed to embody effortlessly. But he knew something of him had died in the explosion at ThutoCo headquarters.

THEY RODE in silence the rest of the way, Moss watching out the window as skyscrapers gave way to an endless sea of tenement housing. What had been hillsides and single-family homes had been bulldozed when the citizens of the world had been forced into the cities, creating the ceaseless concrete and glass world they now inhabited. The rail pulled to a stop, and Gibbs nodded. They disembarked into the Reyes district, a statue of a long-extinct animal towering over the station as they stepped off. Moss stopped to look. The creature was massive, with fins and a fatty nose which curled down over its face. Moss tried to read the plaque under layers of spray-painted tags.

"Elephant seal," he said, and Gibbs turned back.

"You and animals," he said.

"It's just, can you believe this thing used to exist?" Moss asked, staring up at the beast.

"They have clone zoos. You could probably still see one," he offered.

"Not the same. I want to see something like this out where it lived," he said, lost in the thought of hundreds of these creatures galumphing up a hillside.

"They have weird shit off-world," Gibbs noted.

"Something tells me they wouldn't sell us tickets to the colonies," Moss joked.

"Right," Gibbs chuckled. "Let's get this over with."

The streets of Reyes were quiet, populated only with folks heading home after late shifts. They walked for what seemed an interminable time through the sameness, every building a carbon copy of the last. Gibbs seemed to be closely examining all the spray-painted art upon the walls, the only thing which differentiated the concrete rectangles. They stopped where "La Vie B" was written above a window and Gibbs rapped on the glass. They waited. No one came. He knocked again and eventually, a dark-skinned man with a shaved head opened the window suspiciously.

"I don't know you," he said in an accent which Moss did not recognize.

"I'm Che, and this is Floyd. Patchwork sent us," Moss said.

"Don't know no Patchwork," he announced and began to close the window.

"You do," Gibbs insisted.

"Fine," the man said. "Whatcha want?"

"That's it?" Gibbs laughed.

"You'd be surprised how easy 'no' sends people packing," the man explained. His demeanor was cautious but friendly.

"I need to receive a message from Carcer," Moss explained, and the man's face grew grim.

"That'll cost," he said seriously. Moss pulled the motherboard from the satchel. A broad smile crossed the man's lips, exposing teeth which had never seen a dentist. "Patch explained then?"

"Yes," Gibbs put plainly. "May I ask you a question?"

"You may," the man said, perplexed.

"I don't know that accent," he said.

"Not how questions work," the man responded with self-satisfaction.

"What's the accent?" Gibbs pressed, undeterred.

"It's Trinbagonian," the man said, knowing it would mean nothing to them. He got the blank stares he was expecting. "Everyone fled Trinidad and Tobago when the bacteria struck. The island's been clear cut, and the drudges grow sugar and tobacco there now. We keep our culture alive in communities in small pockets of the remaining cities. Same story for a lot of peoples," he said, eyeing them. "You guys bubs? What's that like?"

Moss was surprised by the question. Everyone always assumed they knew what life in the Burbs was like and never asked about it.

"Sheltered," Gibbs answered, hanging his head slightly.

"I'm sure," the man said. "Climb on through."

He stepped back from the window and let them clamber in. It was made easier by stacked cinderblocks piled as stairs. The room was cramped and smelled of incense, and a mattress lay on the floor. Soft steel pan music trickled out of a small speaker beside the bed. The man reached out a hand, and Moss gave over the motherboard.

"Patch didn't want it? Or you procured more?" he asked.

"Neither," Moss admitted.

"He must like you then," the man observed.

"Something like that," Moss said.

"You know the routine here?" he asked.

"No," Moss told him.

"Right. You'll take this," he said, handing Moss a pill in a crumpled paper cup, "and lay down in a stall. Your friend can sit watch outside. Won't need headgear since all you bubs have the implant. We'll sync you with the MI, and you can meet someone in there who can get you the message."

"What's the MI?" Gibbs asked before Moss had a chance.

"Didn't think they had turnip trucks anymore." The man laughed at his own joke, and Gibbs chuckled along. "It's the Mass Illusion, a VR world preferred by the computer artists here."

"Can't be done on a computer in the real world?" Moss asked.

"You think this shit is the real world?" the man chided, looking around the tiny space. "I'm sure it could be, but folks around here prefer this."

"I think a lot of people prefer it," Gibbs observed, and the man tapped a finger to his nose.

"All right," Moss said. "Let's do this."

"Fine by me," the man said and took a key off a board of hooks. "Room nine."

He opened a door at the back of the room and turned to plop

back on his cushion. The door led to a long hallway illuminated with naked red bulbs screwed into makeshift sockets in the ceiling. Doors flanked the hallway with small stools set before them. Some of the stools were occupied by threatening-looking people who no doubt served as protection for the people inside.

"You're armed?" Moss asked, and Gibbs tapped a box at his side which could fold out into a rifle at the push of a button.

"Sure you want to do this?" Gibbs checked.

"We've come this far," Moss answered as he strode to door nine and opened it. The room was small, with a bed and pillow and a small table with a bottle of water. Machinery was mounted above the bed, and a small lamp on the floor lit the space. The room smelled faintly of urine and bleach.

"I'll be out here when you're done," Gibbs said.

"Thanks, you gonna be okay? You bring a tablet or something?" Moss asked, not sure how long this would take.

"I'll be fine. Maybe I'll make friends with the others waiting out here." He smirked. "Failing that, I'll see if I can remember all the lines to a movie."

Moss laughed. "Have fun with that."

"You know I will," he said, snatching the key from Moss's hand and shutting the door in his face. Moss turned and sat on the bed. A green light turned on the machine above. He took a deep breath, swallowed the pill, and gulped some water. The drug worked instantly, and he lay down to keep from falling off the side of the bed.

HE OPENED his eyes in a field of digital daisies under a beautiful blue sky. White wisps of clouds shifted overhead as he leaned up. He felt sick as the world tilted forward, then over and he fell with a thud on the sky. He looked up to see the street and open window he recognized from outside. He glanced back down, and the sky was a puddle full of cigarette butts. His brain hurt, and he reached back to rub his implant as he stood. He was wearing his ThutoCo issued linen pajamas, his name written upside down and backward across his chest. He knew VR worlds sometimes required some acclimation, but this was very different.

He climbed through the window into a ballroom with a checkered floor and elaborate chandeliers with candles topped by purple flames. Naked people covered in body paint to give the illusion of scales moved about the room, drinking champagne and making small talk about the weather. All of them were fit and beautiful, the men all sporting large erections with eyes painted on the tips of their penises. One woman turned, her hair flowing around her as if underwater. She walked over in serpentine steps and looked at Moss with yellow, reptilian eyes.

"You're Che?" she asked dubiously, the words slithering from her lips.

"I am," he said, working hard to stay cool in such unfamiliar surroundings.

"You like my world?" she asked with a sweeping hand gesture.

"Takes some getting used to," Moss told her, not wanting to start off on a lie.

"I'm sure." The "s" slid elongated off her tongue. "A message awaits you?"

"Yes, but I cannot have it traced," Moss said.

"Oh, my dear, nothing in here can be traced, it's a great void," she said. "Please follow me."

He did as they exited through a door which had been a painting moments before. They entered a long hallway of striped walls which shifted like sand. As they walked, he watched her sway, the painted blue scales shifting up and down with the rhythmic movement of her buttocks. She turned to glance over her shoulder, and Moss flushed, averting his gaze.

"You can look. I like that you look," she offered, making Moss even more uncomfortable. He was unaccustomed to overt sexuality, and he did not know how to handle himself. He watched the walls. "Suit yourself," she said, sounding almost wounded. So, he returned to watching her, feeling all the time uneasy.

They turned and walked through the wall into a room of gaudy opulence—gold furniture with red velvet seats, a table set with food Moss had never before seen, and paintings, portraits, and busts on every wall and in every corner. She gestured for him to sit on a long couch, and he did so. She sat beside him, her naked form brushing against his side. He fought an instinct to move away, not wanting to offend. He knew this world wasn't real. It was all a digital dream, but the discomfort remained. He knew Gibbs would mock him for how uncomfortable he was beside a naked woman.

She waved her hands, and a screen appeared. "I've found the message for you. It's deep code, and no one will know. Shall I play it?"

"I would prefer to watch it alone," he said apologetically.

"Understood, but you can't blame a girl for trying." She stood, brushing her body against his as she went, smiling slightly. He wondered if his reaction amused her. It seemed to. She left the room, and he waited. The screen flickered, and a familiar face appeared before him.

"Hey, Moss. Mr. Greene here. Hope this message finds you well," his former ThutoCo boss said. His conversational tone was so forced as to be excruciating, and beads of sweat dotted his hairline. His eyes were terrified under a causal mask. "Your friends back here at work miss you and hope you come back to us real soon. You know you always have a place in engineering."

His eyes constantly shifted off-camera to whoever was coaching him, likely at the barrel of a gun. It pained Moss to know that the man who had helped him fit in at work after his parents were taken was now suffering because of him.

"Your friends here at ThutoCo would love to chat with you. And I mean that—we are friends. You may think you know the people you're mixed up with now, but they are not your friends, they are using you." Mr. Greene was trying to sell it hard now but was failing. The words were coming out hurried and jumbled.

"When they have gotten from you what they want, they will spit you out and leave you on the street. We, on the other hand, want you back. Don't you think it's time you came home?" he asked, his face contorted into an unnatural shape of a smile. Moss's heart broke for the man. All he had ever done was nurture a young man, and now his life was undoubtedly being threatened. Moss knew Mr. Greene had no knowledge of the plan to kill all the employees. He had simply been a middle manager living out his prescribed path. Moss wished he could speak to him. Really speak—not this canned, forced message which would never get Moss to turn himself in.

"And if you need incentives, you know how we love incentives," Greene said in a line which was supposed to be a light-hearted joke, but his body betrayed him, his face contorting to a grim smile.

"Our friends at Carcer wanted you to see this," he continued and looked off-camera once more. The image cut to an image of an ancient woman who Moss did not recognize, gardening in a small chain-link cage. Next to her was a rusted out, corrugated tin building which served as a home. Moss didn't know what he was looking at until another face he knew stepped through the door of the ramshackle home. His curly black hair and mustache were instantly recognizable as Warden Ninety-Nine, the man who had beaten Moss on the roof of ThutoCo HQ. He strode out and looked at the camera with a wicked grin.

He held a baton in a robotic hand and approached the woman from behind, landing a hard blow on her back. Though old, she looked tough and took the unseen hit like someone who was accustomed to abuse. She turned, and he continued to land blow after blow on her body until Moss shut his eyes, unable to watch the pain being inflicted on this person. The sounds of her screams still rang in his ears when the feed cut back to Mr. Greene.

His face was sheet white. Moss realized they must have made him watch it, also. He swallowed and spoke, the words weak, "You might not think you know that woman, but you do. Moss, you do. That's your grandmother. Carcer has her and has agreed to let her go if you just come in for a chat. Please," he was genuine now, begging sincerely for his own life as much as for Sandra's.

"Please come back," the feed cut out. Moss didn't know what to do. He wanted to scream. He looked around the horrible digital room and wanted to wake up.

He slapped his face.

He pressed his eyes closed and then opened them, hoping to be back in his real body.

"I want to get out of here!" he yelled, though it sounded like a plea.

After a moment, the serpentine woman returned, stepping into the room in a sultry stride.

"I want to wake up," Moss insisted.

"That is not the way of things," the woman said, shaking her head, her hair flowing about her. "This is my world, but you can go to one of your own—your personal playground."

He knew how VR worked, but he had always had the option to log out at his whim.

"So, I'm trapped here?" he asked.

"Trapped is such a negative view," she said, cocking her head.

"So, yes?" he pressed.

"It can be your world. You may sleep if you wish."

"Thank you," he said and pressed closed his eyes, willing the program to change his location.

He opened them and was in his Hex—he could sleep here and wake up back in the real world. For a moment, he thought he saw the flash of a man's form in the room like a digital ghost. He blinked but whatever it was, was gone.

"Is this what you want?" he heard Issy—the woman he had been in love with for his whole life—ask. He turned to see her standing in his room in a sheer nightgown, her form clear as day through the slight fabric. He felt manipulated by his own mind. She walked toward him, moving as the scaled woman.

"Not like this," Moss protested.

"Why not?" she asked, playing hurt and putting a hand gently on his chest.

"This isn't real," he said, knowing he could simply will her away, but not yet able to part with her.

"I know you had me as a relief aide, what's different?" she asked, his deep fear made real.

"You know that?" he questioned, hearing the shame in his voice.

"I do," she told him with a smile her real-life counterpart would never give.

She opened her robe, letting it flutter to the floor and puddle at her feet. Every centimeter of her naked body was on display to him, and she twirled, her physical form the perfection of his imagination.

He wanted to grab her, pick her up and throw her on a bed.

He wanted to allow himself this false dream.

He shook his head.

"No," he forced.

"Why?" she pouted, stomping one foot. His unconscious was working hard.

She bit her lip, and he nearly gave in.

"You aren't real," and he did will her away.

He couldn't take this now. Carcer Corp has his grandmother, and he could work to make amends with Issy in real life. Sleeping with her in a dream was pointless, and he needed to return to the world.

His bed slid from the wall, and he lay down.

CHAPTER 3

Moss awoke, back in the small room in Reyes. His mouth was dry and tasted of medicine. He sucked down the remaining water and stood uneasily, his robotic legs making up for a weakened body. He knocked on the door, and he heard the key.

Gibbs swung it open, saying, "I'm your huckleberry."

"What?" Moss snarled, not in the mood for Gibbs' game. "They have my grandma!"

"Who? Carcer?" Gibbs snapped back to reality, his eyes frantic.

Moss leaned up in the bed, his body stiff. "Yes."

"Where?" Gibbs asked, walking into the room and helping Moss to his feet.

"Can't be sure, but I think it's Carcer City," Moss said, rubbing his neck.

Gibbs looked confused. "Where?"

"Ynna told me about it. It's a city-sized prison where people on the outside pay to keep their friends or family alive," Moss explained.

"Oh," Gibbs said, disgust written on his face. "So, it's like—"

Moss cut him off, "We have to get back and tell the others."

"You want to break her out?" Gibbs asked, knowing the answer.

Moss looked at his friend with grim determination. "Yes," he said flatly. "She's the only family member I have left."

"So you think," Gibbs pointed out. "Your memories of your parents were wiped. For all you know, they could still be alive somewhere."

"If they had my parents, they would have used them," Moss said coldly as they entered the small room with the window.

"Bye, Bernard," Gibbs smiled to the man laid out on the mattress.

As they climbed out of the window, Moss said, "So, you did make a friend."

"Naturally," Gibbs said, and once they were out of earshot, "tell me more."

"They made Mr. Greene read the message. He was terrified. I don't want to think what they've done to him since," Moss said, blinking to adjust his eyes in the light of day. He gauged the sun and realized it was close to setting. He had been laying in that room for the better part of a day.

"He was always a good man," Gibbs observed, sadness coating his words.

"Is, he *is* a good man," Moss corrected, more for himself.

"Right," Gibbs said as they walked back to the rail station. "Is there anything we can do for him?"

"No," Moss said, and though it saddened him, he knew there wasn't.

When they reached the station, Moss used his implant to pay.

"Invalid payment," the turnstile shouted from a small speaker.

"Shit, Seti is changing our accounts again," Moss groused. Their eye in the sky would often move their money around when it looked as if someone was closing in on their trail. Moss hopped the turnstile, and Gibbs followed clumsily. He was getting into better shape than he had been in the Burb, but it was taking time, and the baby fat persisted despite Stan's efforts. Stan, the former athlete, was working on getting the two bubs into shape, but he was also teaching them about good food and Gibbs was taking a shine to one more than the other.

"So, where is this city?" Gibbs whispered loudly on the rail train. Moss glanced around, but no one was looking.

"No idea," he answered truthfully. Though he was determined to help his grandmother, no matter the difficulty, the idea of breaking into and out of a prison was not an appealing prospect. Things had been good recently. They had been running low-grade jobs and collecting intel for future use. A job like this was liable to complicate things.

"And how do you suppose we get there?" Gibbs asked.

"I have no fucking clue," Moss hissed. He had been worrying over that problem as well. "Sorry."

"It's fine," Gibbs said, obviously wounded that Moss had snapped.

Moss's voice became quiet and soft, "It's just a lot."

"I know," Gibbs said, putting a hand on his friend's shoulder. "We'll help her."

"If not for me, then for Burn," Moss said. Their former mentor had a relationship with Moss's grandmother, the exact nature of which had never been made clear, though he had his suspicions.

Gibbs looked at his friend with a reassuring smile. "For both of you."

Moss knew Burn would be the selling point to the crew. They might not be inclined to break into the most heavily guarded place on earth just for him, but they would for Burn. Plus, he knew Sandra had brought some of them to the group, and they might be willing to help if they knew she was still alive. It was going to be quite a reveal when they got back.

"Think Patch will be mad?" Gibbs asked.

"About us stealing the motherboard we just got him and trading it?" Moss said. "Yeah, maybe. But hopefully, the intel will be worth it. I know his mom and Burn were close, so maybe he'll be happy to know we can do something in his honor."

"I hope so," Gibbs said, shifting nervously.

"He won't be mad at you. I was the one who did it," Moss said.

"I woke you and made this whole thing happen," Gibbs reminded him.

"He doesn't need to know that, and I'm pretty sure if Judy even remembers, they're only waking up now to rat us out," Moss said.

"Judy doesn't seem like the rat-out type," Gibbs said.

"Truer words," Moss noted.

IT WAS sunset by the time they exited the station, the remaining sun coating the clouds crimson. Gibbs said, "You think we should pick something up? Giorgio's by way of apology?"

"Yeah, that's a good idea," Moss agreed as they turned to head toward the pizza shop.

Something wasn't right. They could both feel it. The street seemed too quiet, and something was off. Moss gripped the handle of his pistol, and they turned back toward the apartment. A Carcer drone buzzed by overhead. Moss pulled up the collars of his trench coat and Gibbs the hood of his sweatshirt. They moved into the alleyway quickly, heads low. They all knew this was the spot, the vantage point to check out the building if something seemed amiss. They skulked forward, and Moss peaked around the corner to see the building. His heart was pounding, his eyes wide with terror as he surveyed the scene. Red lights flashing, streetcars and flighted cars surround the building. What looked to be nearly one hundred officers stood in the area, weapons trained at the building. Drones circled and buzzed like a swarm of locusts. Gibbs looked briefly from over Moss's shoulder.

"No," he cried, and Moss shoved him back, hissing a shush. "What are we going to do?" Gibbs whimpered.

"For now, see what we see. Later, we help them," Moss said, more pragmatic than he would have expected of himself in such a moment. They peered around again, as little happened. The quiet was unnerving. Moss expected gunfire and explosions, but none came.

Seti, Moss tried communicating through his implant. No response. He knew she would have warned him if she could, would have reached out. The reality that they may have gotten to her too was terrifying. There were other crews, but Moss had no way of reaching out to them and going around asking would get him killed.

Then, from the roof of the building, he heard a scream, a gut-wrenching sound of terror as a body flew off the top. Chicken Thumbs hollered in fear as he flailed toward the ground before erupting in blood on the pavement below. Gibbs stifled a scream. Officers rushed to the body, peeling it from the street. It took all of Moss's resolve not to rush out, to pull his weapon and try to kill as many as he could before they got him. But he didn't, knowing he had to wait if he was to be any help to his friends. Then he saw him. Warden Ninety-Nine stepped out on the lip of the roof, loudspeaker in his robotic hand.

"Clean that up," he announced to the officers below, who were already at work. "Get the wagon ready. We have them."

Moss could not see his face clearly from this distance, but the arrogance and pride were clear in his voice. The front door to the building opened, and large Carcer drudges emerged. Stan, Patchwork, Judy, and Grimy were slung, limp over the shoulders of the machines. Moss heard Gibbs shift, and he had his Kingfisher out and pointed in a flash.

He turned to see Ynna, hair wet, wearing a dirty and ripped bathrobe, holding a hand over Gibbs's mouth. She looked to Moss, a finger over her lips. She wore an expression Moss had never seen from her before—fear. Even when they thought they were going to die in the basement of ThutoCo, she had been stoic and ready, but now, she looked sad and scared.

"Fan out, we are still missing some," Warden Ninety-Nine announced from the roof. Ynna cocked her head, and the three ran as the officers began to assemble. They had all had the escape routes drilled into them, and Moss knew which way Ynna was leading them. They rushed to the carpet shop which had an escape van parked at its rear. A bell rang as they pushed through the door, and the shopkeeper nodded, understanding the context and opened the door to the back quickly.

"Good luck," he told them, handing Ynna keys as they passed into the alley beyond. They hopped into the van and Ynna started it up, the ancient engine choking to life.

"It happened so fast," Ynna said pitifully, letting her head drop.

As they pulled onto the road, Moss asked, "You were in the shower?"

"Yes," she said, her eyes darting back and forth, looking for pursuers.

"Lucky," Gibbs observed.

"Escapees through the vents?" Moss asked.

"Yes, just like in a movie," Ynna said as she drove them quickly away from the neighborhood.

"Seriously," Gibbs began.

"Lucky, I know," she snapped, driving slowly and obeying traffic laws, trying not to make it obvious that a human driver was operating the vehicle. A non-computer driver would be a dead giveaway. "We're fucked," she said.

"No," Gibbs tried.

"No, we're fucked," Ynna repeated. "I tried Seti, but they either shut down comms, or they got her, too."

"Also froze our accounts," Moss added, remembering the turnstile.

"Shit!" Ynna screamed, pounding the steering wheel. "Get anything from that message?" Ynna asked, knowing why the two had been absent.

"Nothing helpful now, they have my grandmother, too," Moss told her. Ynna blinked with confusion.

Ynna looked surprised. "Sandra's alive?"

"Yes," Moss said.

"Carcer City?" she asked, turning right, away from the now compromised safe house.

Trying to shake the images from his mind, Moss said, "It certainly looked that way."

"You guys," Gibbs interrupted as though he couldn't hold his tongue any longer.

"What?" Ynna asked.

"Chicken Thumbs just died," he stated in a quiet, heart-broken voice.

"We fucking know it," Ynna said, sadness manifesting as rage. "He was a good person, but he was never meant for this. Burn had a soft spot for him, but there was nothing we could do."

"I know, it just," Gibbs trailed off.

Moss knew why it upset Gibbs so much. "You're not like him."

"No, I mean—" Gibbs protested hollowly. "Thank you."

"Should serve as a reminder to all of us to keep our heads screwed on straight. I'm sure he tried to run for it and felt the wrath of that prick who shot me," Ynna said, her blood up, eyes red. She never took her eyes from the road. She didn't look at them. Moss wondered if she resented that they were the two she had ended up with at a time like this.

"So, what now?" Moss asked.

"Get some clothes, some gear and find an ally," she stated.

"We're fucked for money," Moss reminded her.

"Shit, right," she said, looking at the tattered bathrobe.

"Not entirely," Gibbs said with a hint of pride.

"What?" Moss and Ynna asked in unison.

"Figured this could happen one day, so I put some money on a card just in case," he explained, a slight smile crossed Ynna's mouth.

"I've never liked you more than I do right now," she said.

"Must not have liked me all that much then," he said, shooting a look at Moss.

"Really want to pull that thread?" Ynna asked as they descended a hill, the walls of the city coming into view far in the distance. The city faced the ocean to the west and extended for hundreds of kilometers to the north and south but did not reach that far to the east. There were only a few districts before the wall. A massive concrete structure stood with guard posts and fields of misters on the other side, spraying a liquid to keep the bacteria at bay. There was a massive tunneled train system which ferried people to and from the other cities and quarantine customs checkpoints for the new arrivals.

The van pulled through a tunnel onto a large suspension bridge which used to cross a body of water which had been covered over a generation earlier and served as a massive open-air market where people lived in rooms behind their storefronts.

Moss looked beyond the market to all the ThutoCo Burbs, towering like white beehives in the distance. They had been his whole world for so long, and now they seemed like a distant memory.

"We could save ourselves a lot of trouble and go back," Gibbs said, catching Moss's glance.

"That would be a short, one-way trip," Moss said, not inclined to joke.

"Yes, it would," Ynna agreed. "Gibbs, how much money you got?"

"Not much, a couple million," Gibbs said.

"It'll do," Ynna said. "We'll stop in Old Oak and then head to the Wall Burg."

"Are we—" Moss began to ask.

She cut him off. "No, we are going to see Jo." He had thought perhaps they were going to find Issy and her dad, and while he wanted to see her, he did not want to put her in peril.

"She's gonna be pissed," Gibbs said. "Patch calls her every day. They are really close."

"No one on earth is going to be more inclined to help us than a mother whose son is in peril," Ynna noted, a twinge of cold jealousy in her voice. Keeping up with the computerized traffic was difficult for a person and Ynna seemed relieved as they pulled off the freeway. After a few minutes, they were parking at Jo's bar.

As they stepped through the door, Jo looked up at them, appraised Ynna quickly and yelled, "No!" She slapped the bar with rage and sadness. "I told Burn to keep him safe, he promised. I should never have let him stay!" Her eyes welled.

"Jo," Ynna began.

"No, I don't want to hear it!" she screamed, all eyes in the bar on her, save a few too transfixed by their lenscreens.

"He's okay, we just need help," Ynna pleaded.

"Don't tell me he's okay if he ain't," she said and upturned a whiskey bottle into her mouth.

"Well," Ynna began, and Jo put the bottle down, pure misery replacing the anger.

"Come on upstairs," she said and looked at Ynna. "I'll get you some new duds."

They followed her up the wooden stairs to a couple of doors where she whispered, "little ones sleeping in there, come on." She led them into the room, which served as her office and bedroom—a desk with papers on one side and a bed on the other. Kids' toys littered the floor. "Tell me," she said as she indicated for the boys to sit on the bed.

"Carcer arrested Patchwork," Ynna said, not mincing words.

"I suppose it was bound to happen someday," his mother admitted. "Boy's been hacking things he shouldn't since he was knee-high."

"Must be why he's so good," Gibbs offered.

"I don't know this one," Jo said, pulling out a cardboard box with "lost and found" scrawled on the side and handing it over to Ynna. "Here," she offered, and Ynna began rummaging.

"I'm Gibbs," he said, "another friend of your son's."

"Yeah, you would be," she said, and Gibbs gave her a puzzled expression. "He always did run with nerd boys like you."

Gibbs chuckled, "Dead to rights."

"Ugh, these pants were pissed in," Ynna complained, dropping the jeans she was holding.

"Ain't running a charity here," Jo snapped.

"Sorry," Ynna said, returning to the box.

"Suppose I'll be hearing from Carcer soon myself," Jo said.

"Almost certainly," Moss agreed. "They will charge him high and low, and as next of kin, you'll be expected to pay up."

"This fucking system," Jo snorted. "Live under the thumb of

the rich, then pay them when they accuse you. Keep the poor poor. It's sick."

"We are trying to do something about it. So was your son," Moss offered.

"I know it," she admitted. "He knows I'm proud of him. All us who served, fought, and bled for corporate greed and were thrown to the street, we all appreciate what you kids do."

"Thank you," Ynna said, holding up a checkered skirt which looked similar to what she normally wore. Moss felt guilty accepting praise from a woman who had just lost her son into the system they were working so hard to fight.

"They gonna take him to C City?" Jo asked. Gibbs was watching Ynna pull the skirt on under her bathrobe. "Give the girl some privacy," Jo admonished.

"Yeah, he's a man of great fucking subtlety," Ynna laughed. "They will probably take him there, question him."

"Torture, you mean," Jo said, darkness in her voice.

"We are going to try to get there before that happens," Ynna explained and turned to pull on a shirt. Moss noticed the scar on Ynna's back—the exit wound from when Warden Ninety-Nine had shot her. Grimy had offered to smooth the skin, to leave no trace of the event. Ynna had said no, she wanted the reminder of all that had happened that day.

"We also learned," Moss added, "that they have Sandra. I assume you know her, too?"

Jo was shocked, her mind racing to try and understand. "No shit. Burn drowned himself for months after she died—after we thought she died, anyhow."

"Can you tell us about it?" Gibbs coaxed.

"You knew Burn, weren't much of a talker, except to cuss," Jo said, sitting at the chair beside her desk. "Just said she died how she lived, fighting for what she believed. There was one night where he was hardly conscious. He said he left her to die.

That she made him. I asked about it when he was clear-headed, but he just said he must have been drunk. Don't know much more than that. Sad to think he died with that on his soul."

"We can take solace in the fact that he died the way he thought she did, fighting for what he believed in," Moss said, more to himself than the room, but Jo nodded.

"That's something, anyway," she said quietly. "So, how you going to get my boy back?"

"We need to get outside the wall," Ynna said. She had pulled a black tee shirt with "Nirvana" written across the front over a long-sleeved gray shirt. She had set her microdyed hair to black and was pulling it into pigtails with loose twine from the floor. Gibbs was staring at her in a way Moss had never seen his friend look at anything.

"You need a hookup?" Jo asked.

"Yes," Ynna admitted, "and some shoes I can borrow?"

"I can provide both," Jo said, standing and sliding open a locked closet door. "Have to keep my shoes locked away. My daughter kept trying to put them on and falling all over the place."

"Cute," Ynna said with a slight smile.

"Not as cute as it sounds," Jo corrected. "You heading to the Burg from here?"

"We are if that's where you know someone," Ynna said, pulling on a pair of black combat boots.

"Shoulda known you'd go for my military gear," Jo said, raising an eyebrow.

Ynna replied with quiet pride, "Burn taught me well."

"Sure did. And breaking into C City is the same kind of dumbfuck plan Burn would have hatched," Jo said, a hint of a smile on her lips.

Ynna smirked. "I'll take that as a compliment."

"It was meant that way," Jo said, smiling at the young woman. "My friend can get you out, but I'm sure it'll cost."

"We have a little money," Ynna said, nodding almost imperceptibly at Gibbs.

"You'll need more than a little," Jo said. "Tell him I sent you though, maybe he'll remember he owes me one and give y'all a discount—though I doubt it."

"So, who is this guy?" Moss asked.

"Most folks just call him Ferret. One of those guys who gets people what they need and disappears when there's trouble," Jo explained.

"Sounds like our kind of guy," Moss said.

"Oh, he'll cozy right up, but don't buy it. Man like that'll sell you down the river without a moment's thought," she warned.

"As long as it's not to Carcer," Ynna said.

"Trust me, he wants less to do with them than you do. He works out of a shithole bar called the Gem. Give him this," Jo said, writing a little note on the back of a business card. "That will get you a sit-down, but the rest is up to you."

"Thank you," Ynna said, taking the card. "We'd be lost in the woods without you."

"Don't think for a second you're out of the woods," Jo warned. "And don't come back here without my boy, lest you want one less head on your shoulders."

"We'll get him back," Moss promised. "And we'll bring Sandra by just for good measure."

"Would be nice to see that old broad again." Jo smiled. "Now get out of here."

Moss stood to leave, Gibbs still rooted to the spot, gazing at Ynna.

"What's wrong with you?" Jo shouted and threw a slipper at him, striking him in the chest and returning him to the world. "I don't know where you find these ones," she said to Ynna.

"He came packaged with the useful one," Ynna joked, and Moss saw his friend was hurt by the comment. Moss knew his friend was a good man and would prove himself useful but wished he would stop acting like a little kid.

"Can I ask you one more favor?" Ynna asked sheepishly.

Jo shot her a knowing look. "I got a couple of pieces behind the bar and a few boxes of ammo, but this is a loan, you hear?"

"Heard," Ynna said in a way reminiscent of Patchwork.

"The Burg is dangerous, so you may need it," Jo said.

"The Legion?" Moss asked nervously.

"Nah, it's Hoplite territory, lucky for you. Willis told me you had some run-ins with those bikers," she said.

"Yeah, well, at least the Hoplites don't want us dead," Moss said.

"Yet," Jo forewarned.

CHAPTER 4

Moss and Gibbs waited by the van as Ynna picked out a gun. "What the fuck?" Moss asked harshly.

"Sorry," Gibbs said and meant it. "She's just—it's just—I don't know."

"We can't keep having this conversation. It's getting real old," Moss told him.

"I know, it's how—" he began, and Moss cut him off.

"Don't tell me it's how you respond to stress. Just get your head out of your ass and be the man who brought me to this city."

"Right," Gibbs said. "Sorry."

"Stop apologizing and change," Moss scolded.

"Okay," Gibbs said, hanging his head.

Ynna stepped from the bar on slightly wobbling legs, cigarette between her fingers and rifle with attached grenade launcher in the other.

"She had that behind the bar?" Moss asked, astonished.

"Sure did," Ynna said, the scent of whiskey radiating from her. "You dipshits ready to hit the road?"

"Of course, we have one of the only cars in the city without autonav," Gibbs complained, watching Ynna walk on unsteady legs.

"You don't get to talk," Ynna said, pointing two derisive fingers trailing smoke.

"You good to drive?" Moss checked.

"Can you operate a vehicle?" Ynna over-enunciated her words.

"Not really. I mean, Stan has been—" Moss began. Ynna shot him a withering look. "Not really, no."

"Then you can shut the fuck up," she said. "Let's go meet a ferret."

THEY CLIMBED into the van and rolled toward the wall. Moss sat in the passenger seat beside Ynna who now drove much less cautiously. Gibbs sat in the back and was gently snoring after only a few minutes. She turned on some thudding electronic music but made it quiet, turning to Moss.

"What the fuck is with him?" she asked, spraying ash from the top of her cigarette out of the window. The streets of Old Oak were shoddy and tight, homes built into every available space. The congestion only became worse as they moved closer to the wall.

"It's a huge change. We were sheltered for so long, know nothing of how it works out here. We've been pampered and coddled and have no relevant skills. It's a hard adjustment," Moss defended.

"You don't seem to be struggling," Ynna pointed out.

"People are different," Moss said, knowing the hollow platitude wouldn't work on Ynna.

"Lame," she said, flicking the butt to explode in embers on the street. "Listen, when we get to Ferret, you need to do the talking."

"All right," Moss said, his surprise evident in his voice.

"Apparently, he's sexist," Ynna said, making no attempt to hide her contempt.

"Of course, he is," Moss said.

Ynna smiled a little. "Right? Just what we need."

"I mean, it was bound to get worse," Moss joked.

"Sure, things really aren't bad enough for us," Ynna said, wearing a broad grin now.

"Nope. Carcer has our friends and my grandmother, who I didn't even know was alive. We have no money. We somehow have to get to Carcer City, which is probably not an easy feat. Oh, and once we get there, we somehow have to break into a city designed to keep people in," Moss said, laughing at the insanity of it all as well.

Ynna lit another cigarette and offered one to Moss, which he accepted gratefully. He had only smoked a few times since leaving the Burb, but now seemed like the right time. She produced a small bottle from a pocket and threw it to Moss. He took a quick swig.

"Never ends," Ynna observed, returning to solemnity.

"No, it doesn't," Moss agreed.

"Have one victory at least," Ynna said.

Moss agreed. "That we did. Even did some good."

"Right."

"Think we will be able to pull this one off?" Moss asked.

"Get them out of C City? Don't know. Shit, Moss, we don't even know if that's where they are being taken," she reminded him.

"Yeah," Moss said, the weight of it landing heavily upon him. "And it's just the three of us."

"Two of us, more like," Ynna said, taking a final swig and chucking the bottle out the window. She was driving more slowly now, the roads so narrow that the van could barely move without scarring the sides. She had to stop for every person on the road until they ducked into a doorway. She honked at stray dogs who lazed in the street and flashed her lights at the alley-cats, the citizens of this district unwilling to spend their money on animal care. As they moved further from the center of the city, the poverty became more oppressive.

Here, people simply built homes with found material or squeezed themselves into the available spaces. Scaffolding was repurposed, covered in corrugated metal and bolted to the inside of the wall to create a horizontal community. Ladders were strapped with cable ties, rope or tape to the front so people could climb into their precarious houses, and hundreds of extension cords were pulled from the other side of the street.

Ynna parked on the aptly named Wall Road, and they got out.

"Should we leave him?" Ynna asked of Gibbs who was still asleep in the car.

"Yeah, let him rest. We'll just say he was guarding the car," Moss said with a chuckle. "Anyway, he was up all night, making sure I was safe in a VR."

"Nice of him," Ynna said. "Think he'll be pissed when he wakes up?"

"Nah," Moss said.

There was very little street between the wall-face homes and the businesses across. A single lane wide enough for the rick-shaws which pushed one another out of the way was all that divided the two sides. People looked out of the windows of their homes to the street below, chatting and shouting.

"Real hummus sold here," one woman shouted to them from above. "No vats here, real chickpeas! Come up for sample."

"Doing chemistry art up here, come take a look," another person offered from a dimly lighted window leaking smoke. They ignored all the offers and walked down the street. Nearly every storefront seemed to be either a bar or grocer, alternating back and forth between oppressive light and the dim. They read name after tavern name, looking for the Gem.

As it always seemed to after the sun had set, the sky opened up, and the rain began, light at first as if a heavy wet fog was settling into place. Everyone in the street felt the shift, and soon most were going about their business under awnings.

One building shone brighter onto the street than the others, and as they approached, they saw why. It was a massively tall affair, built of glass and clear plastic only. Each successive floor became darker and more crowded.

The ground floor was brightly lit, serving craft beer about which the locals could brag. The next few floors were populated with bars serving cocktails for the after-work crowd, those who would likely rather be caught dead than admit to their work friends that they live in the Burg.

The several top layers were dimly lit with flashing lights and dance music which thudded dully down to the streets. The name Gem was projected on the front of the circular structure, the word frenetically dancing about the front.

Moss looked at all the people moving about on all the layers.

"We should have asked what Ferret looks like," Moss said.

"I did," Ynna said.

"Should have known," Moss admitted, "and?"

"He looks like a fucking weasel apparently," Ynna said with a snort.

"I guess I shouldn't be surprised," Moss said as they approached the front door where a drudge sat, serving as a bouncer. It sat on a stool and tilted its metal head at them as they approached.

"One hundred each," it said in the factory default voice.

"Steep," Ynna said, pulling Gibb's money card.

"Sneaky," Moss said.

"Stole it the second he mentioned it," Ynna bragged. Moss smiled.

"I would expect nothing less," Moss said, and Ynna bowed with flair. The drudge scanned the card.

"Bartenders are going to love you," the drudge said sarcastically in its electric monotone. "Cool kids think you're so hip paying in this old-timey way, but it's really just inconvenient."

"They programmed you to have a fucking attitude but didn't give you a voice, really nice," Ynna observed, smirking at the machine. It groaned—an unnatural, synthetic sound.

"Really clever. Think you're the first to point that out?" the drudge asked, handing the card back. "Just get in there before I beat your ass."

As they walked through the door, Ynna hissed over her shoulder, "Prick."

"What did you say?" the drudge asked, standing from its unnecessary stool. Moss grabbed her by the shoulder and pulled her up the stairs. She was snickering. They walked up level after level of twisted staircase, sticking out like sore thumbs on the first several floors. The people sitting and drinking, though about Moss's age, looked like kids in their suits and dresses, sipping at expensive glowing drinks. The music from the floors above grew louder, and they could look up through the steamed floor to awkwardly moving feet dancing along. "She said he'd be on six," Ynna yelled to Moss over her shoulder.

"Seems like an odd place for an office," Moss said, before adding, "of this nature,"

"Safety in the public nature of it, I guess," Ynna offered.

"Doesn't get more public than this," Moss said. Ynna nodded. No one seemed even to notice them on the sixth floor. Everyone just continued to dance while the DJ with a video screen over his face played the repetitive music the crowd loved. They all moved and gyrated, a sweaty mass of humanity, too focused on themselves or their partners to notice much else.

They pushed toward the tables, noticing a gaunt man with matted blond hair reclining at the back of the room, watching with tiny, suspicious eyes. Ynna handed the business card to Moss as they approached, and he placed it on the table in front of Ferret. He took the card lazily and read it, flipping it back and forth as though it were written in a foreign language. Even Moss could tell the effects of Zcode when he saw it, the man's eyes rolled from the card up to them.

"So, you know Jo?" he asked, his tongue moving leadenly in his mouth.

"I do," Moss said, puffing up his shoulders in affected masculinity.

"And what could you want with me?" he asked, his head listing.

"A way out?" Moss said, playing it coy.

"Out of this existence? Go back to the street, anyone can help you there," Ferret said, and slid the card back across the table, knocking into several half-drank drinks.

"No," Moss said, letting a serious tone coat the word. "Out of this city."

"Oh," Ferret said, blinking his eyes to attention, seeming to see them for the first time. "That is a different prop—prep —*thing* altogether," he fumbled.

"Jo said you were the man to talk to," Moss tried stroking his ego. It worked, Ferret grinning and taking a sip from one of the glasses.

"I am!" he announced.

"Good," Moss said.

"But isn't cheap," he furrowed his brows. He enunciated each word. "It is not cheap."

"How not cheap?" Moss asked.

49

"Very," he said with wicked pride.

"We've got a couple million," Moss said, and the man laughed, some remaining drink sloshing from his mouth.

"That won't get you across the street," he explained, "and it'll be more on the other side, depending on where you are going."

"Does it matter where we are going?" Moss asked.

"Not to me," Ferret told him.

"Good," Moss said. "We are in a rush, is there anything we can do to lower the price?"

"You have finally asked a relevant question." He pointed a finger on a hand, seemingly working independently. He ran his eyes over Ynna slowly. "Nothing this one can do for me," he said with disgust. You could be pretty if you tried," he told her before adding, "tried a lot."

She clicked her tongue against her gritted teeth but said nothing. Moss was grateful Jo had warned them about his nature.

"What can we do?" Moss asked.

Ferret's appraised them slowly, the bags beneath his eye a dark purple in the dim room. "Jo says you're okay, then I suppose I can trust you with a favor. And if you fail, you die, and it costs me nothing."

"Fine," Moss said. "And doing this favor for you would pay our passage? We are in a rush."

"Doesn't pay to be in a hurry," the man observed.

"Be that as it may—" Moss began, and Ferret looked upon him with derision.

"All right fancy pants, you can do this thing for me this very moment and leave tonight," he said. "There is a man down the road who has begun taking my business. I need you to ask him to stop, if you take my meaning?"

"We are not assassins," Moss said, and the Ferret raised his hands innocently.

"I simply asked you to make him stop," he reiterated. "How you go about that is none of my business."

"Right," Moss said, ready to be done with this conversation. "Who's the man?"

"Just down the way. Place called the Grindstone. The prick calls himself Powers, the fucking arrogance," he slurred.

Moss turned, seeing the ire in Ynna's face. "We'll be back," Moss told the man and pulled Ynna away.

They hurried through the crowd and moved quickly down the stairs. "Don't have time for fucking side quests," Ynna hissed.

"Should count ourselves lucky that he's willing to bargain, we need the money," Moss said.

"I know," Ynna admitted, her voice still hard. "I don't mind killing some prick."

"Me neither," Moss acknowledged, "but I didn't want him to think it was that easy."

"Smart," Ynna said with a smile. "Wouldn't mind putting a bullet in that asshole's head, too."

"We need him," Moss said before adding, "for now."

Ynna grinned.

CHAPTER 5

They checked on Gibbs who had shifted and was now stretched out across the back seats.

Ynna rolled her eyes at him and mocked, "So helpful."

"Hopefully we won't need the extra gun," Moss said, shifting nervously.

"Let's just get this shit over with," Ynna said, slinging the rifle across her back, careful to close the door quietly. They hustled quickly down the road to the Grindstone, a seedy bar stinking of spilled beer. The bar was populated with bikers from the Hoplites MC, the telltale vests a dead giveaway. They approached the bar where a beefy, bald man looked at them with exhaustion.

"Place isn't for you," he told them.

"Here to see Powers," Ynna said, ignoring his comment.

"Oh, yeah?" he asked, licking his lips. "And what do I get?"

"This one will give you a blow job," Ynna said, hooking a thumb to Moss.

The bartender smirked. "Yeah, fuck you, too, then. Powers is in the back," he said, pointing to a door flanked by two more bikers, watching a TV in the corner.

"Thanks," Moss whispered sarcastically to Ynna as they stepped away.

"Gotta know how to talk to these dimwits," she said with pride. Approaching the thugs, she said, "Here to see Powers."

"What's that to me?" one said, turning his tribal tattoo covered face to them.

"Nothing, I guess," she said and stepped right passed him, swinging the door open.

"Hey!" the other shouted and grabbed her by the wrist. She countered him in a flash, spinning his arm and pressing him to the wall as the man in the office looked up from a screen in his desk.

Moss raised his hands and spoke to the man, feeling the press of a gun barrel against his temple, "Powers, we would like a word."

The man behind the desk stood, the suit he wore stretched tight from the musculature beneath. He had a long, pointed mustache and wore sunglasses, though the room was poorly lit.

"Let them enter," he ordered the guards and Moss felt the gun pull away as Ynna loosened her grip. They stepped in and Powers waved a hand, the door swinging closed behind them at his command. It was just the three of them in the room now, and Moss considered pulling his Kingfisher and being done with it before realizing how foolish a move that would be.

"We hear you're a man on the rise," Moss ingratiated. Ynna shot him a quizzical look but played along.

"The type of man who can get things done," she added.

"You heard right, though you have me at a loss, I don't normally admit strangers," he said, walking to them with an extended hand.

"Che and Marley," Moss said, and they all shook hands with cautious courtesy.

"And I presume there is something I can do for you?" he suggested.

"Something we can do for you," Ynna said, picking up on Moss's plan.

"Even better," he said, clapping his hands.

"Comes with a price," Moss added.

"Everything comes with a price," Powers said thoughtfully. Moss noticed the image on the screen in the desk—full-body scans of both he and Ynna with the augments and mods highlighted. He saw his mechanical legs which looked real to the naked eye but appeared clearly in the scan and his neural implant at the base of his skull. It was larger than he realized wrapping in and around his brain. Ynna was a mess of upgrades, different spots glowing all over the scan.

"We can work out an exchange perhaps?" Ynna suggested.

"Depends both on what you have and what you want," Powers said, all business. "What is it that you want?"

"Passage to the outside," Moss said.

"Now that, I can provide," Powers said with a crocodile smile, displaying a mouth of gold-coated teeth. "And what is it that you can offer me?"

Moss lowered his voice ominously. "A warning."

"If it's about that fucking badger, I already know," he said with a dismissive wave of his hand.

"You know he wants you dead?" Ynna pressed.

"Him among many," Powers said, disappointment in his tone. "I got excited when you made short work of the paid help, but you obviously have nothing."

Ynna crossed her arms and planted her feet. "We were asked to kill you."

"But you didn't and couldn't," he said, pulling his nose up at the bridge, revealing an implanted mesh in the nostrils. "If you so much as thought about raising a weapon in here this room would fill with a neurotoxic gas so quickly you would be bleeding from your eyes before you could even swing that thing from your back. I'm sorry you came all this way for nothing, truly."

Ynna offered in a desperate gambit. "What if we do him?"

Powers' lip turned up slightly. "That might be worth something, though a double-cross is so patently obvious," he said. "And you wouldn't make it out of the Gem alive. Half those patrons are guards."

"That's it! So obvious," Ynna said, slapping Moss's shoulder.

"And if we could?" Moss asked.

"You kill that sack, and you'll have your passage and a new friend," he offered. "Something tells me you would love nothing more," he said to Ynna. "But he will be expecting it."

Moss and Ynna left the Grindstone with a new goal.

"Think Jo will be pissed?" Moss asked.

"Doubt it," Ynna replied. "Whatever she gets from him, she can get from Powers. With our help and Hoplite allies, he'll be running the Burg in no time. That can only make Jo's life easier. Plus, this is all assuming the second part."

"Oh, right, the other bit," Moss chuckled as they approached the van. Ynna opened the rear passenger door, Gibbs' head flopping out before he woke up with a start.

"Oh, man," he said, rubbing his neck. "What's up? I miss anything?"

"We met with Jo's contact, and now we need to kill him," Ynna explained.

"He deserve it?" Gibbs asked.

"Does it matter? He's our key to rescuing our friends from torture and death," Ynna said.

"Pretty sure he's a kingpin surrounded by thugs who plague these streets," Moss explained.

"Fine," Gibbs said, grabbing his rifle box. "What's the plan?"

"Moss is gonna take on the two bottom floors, and I'm going to deal with Ferret. You'll be our eyes and make sure nothing sneaks up on us," Ynna explained.

"Still keep that taser on you?" Moss asked, and it was in his hand in a moment.

"Two floors?" Gibbs asked dubiously.

Moss shot him a coy smile.

THEY APPROACHED THE DRUDGE BOUNCER, and it groaned and rolled its robotic head impatiently.

"You're back?" it asked.

"We missed you." Ynna chuckled, pressing her cybernetic hand to the machine, one of her eyes going black. The machine stuttered and shook slightly. "We could really use Patchwork right about now," she muttered as she worked the hack on the drudge. Moss and Gibbs stood watch; a gaggle of young people approached.

"Is there, like, a cover charge?" one girl asked. The group of one guy and three girls were dressed for dancing and seemed not to notice what was happening.

"Nope, go on in," Gibbs said with a wave of his hand.

"Great," she said, and as they moved passed, one turned back to watch for a moment.

"They don't give repairmen uniforms anymore?" She giggled in a suggestively superior tone.

"We're freelance," Moss told her and waved them on as Gibbs had. They moved on, but he turned to Ynna. "Running short on time," he said.

"These things are designed not to be hacked," Ynna snarled.

"It's just—" Moss began.

"It'll take as long as it takes," Gibbs interrupted.

"Exactly," Ynna agreed thankfully.

Moss ordered, "Get up to a roof and find a good vantage point."

Gibbs turned quickly to find a way up one of the nearby buildings. An older man approached them cautiously.

"Good evening," he said to Moss, glancing over to Ynna.

"Evening," Moss said graciously.

"Can you tell me if this is where the local brew fest is taking place?" he asked, stroking a well-trimmed beard.

"It is. First floor," Moss guessed with confidence. The man did not budge.

"And can you tell me where the hops were grown on any of the particular beers?" he asked. He seemed kind and simply curious, but Moss was not in the mood, worried he might get suspicious if he stood there too long.

"All the information regarding the brews will be prominently displayed inside," Moss said, pointing.

"And how much to enter?" he asked.

"Our drudge is offline for maintenance so you can simply head on in," Moss said, pointing a second time and hearing the annoyance in his own voice.

"Lucky timing for me," the man said and went inside.

"Seriously!" Moss barked.

"I'm getting close," Ynna snapped.

"They're going to have to start paying me if I do this much longer," Moss said.

"Command input?" the drudge said, and Ynna commanded the machine through the nodes in her fingertips.

Synchronization complete, Moss heard through his implant. His brain began receiving data from the machine as it began walking into the bar.

"This was smart," Ynna observed.

"Thanks, stole the idea from the desk—full-body scan on entry," he said.

She nodded. "I noticed that, too."

"You've got a lot of augs," Moss noted.

"You're one to talk! You're all augment from the knee down," Ynna cried, following the drudge. "Anyway, we can discuss the line between man and machine when we get out of here with our hides."

"You mean *if* we get out of this," Moss corrected, and Ynna turned back with a devilish grin.

She chuckled. "Nah, we've gotten out of worse."

Moss saw clean scans as they passed the first few floors and he stopped on the fifth, getting the readout of the concealed weapons in his mind.

"I'll wait," he told Ynna who nodded.

"Good luck," she said with a two-finger salute. Moss walked out to the dancefloor, gripping his Kingfisher under his coat. He clicked it over to non-lethal. He listened, hearing the sound of the drudge's heavy footfalls in his mind. They stopped at the top of the stairs, the drudge waiting just out of sight as commanded. It's microphone still able to pick up the conversation but filtering out the dance music.

I have no reports of anything noteworthy down the street, Moss heard Ferret say.

We did it quietly, Ynna replied.

And your handler, where's he? Ferret condescended.

Didn't make it, Ynna explained.

So, a ticket for one then? Ferret asked. *Providing you have proof of the deed being done.*

Moss knew this was his moment. He stepped forward and pressed his weapon into the back of one of the armed dancers and pulled the trigger. The electric shock coursed through the man and he fell to the floor, vibrating wildly.

"I think he's overdosed," Moss shouted over the music, and everyone around moved aside, Moss hiding among the throng.

"Shit," he heard another of the guards say as they rushed to his aid. "Make some room!" He shouted, gesturing madly for the dancers to disperse. Moss heard the gunshot from above, and people began to shout and run for the exits. The guards were all gathered around their fallen comrade, looking up in shock as Moss pulled his weapon.

He fired.

It was almost too easy with them all gathered in shock. Two hit the floor before the others got wise to what was happening. The flashing lights, pounding beat, and confusion gave Moss cover to move as the three remaining guards pulled their weapons. One pointed a gun at the fleeing crowd, poised to take them all out as long as it meant killing Moss as well.

"Shit," Moss exclaimed, firing his weapon at the guard and separating from the mob of bodies. The guard fell as Moss ducked behind a table which shattered into pieces as the other two opened fire on him. He kept moving, allowing his weapon to cool.

Glass rained down on him as the two guards moved closer. He checked his battery. Enough for one more shot. He got to his knees and dashed for the next table, bullets whizzing around him and exploding the floor and glass wall beyond him. He felt hot pain as a bullet grazed his head.

He smelled blood and singed hair.

The gunfire stopped as the two hid behind another table while they reloaded. Moss moved to another table while they were distracted, looking at the battery. Still only enough for one shot.

He remembered standing with Stan before a weapon rack, anything he could want on offer.

"Want to upgrade?" Stan had asked. Moss had simply shaken his head, happy to use the weapon which had gotten him that far. He regretted that decision now. If he got out of this alive, he would most certainly upgrade to a better weapon, or at least something with better battery life. The two guards popped up, trying to get a fix on Moss.

He pulled the trigger, and the blue light zipped across the room, sending the guard to the floor while the other wheeled to take aim. As he raised his weapon, his neck burst open with a spray of blood as a massive round from Gibbs' rifle passed through him. He clutched at his throat, blood cascading down his body.

Moss gave a thumbs up to the window as he ran upstairs.

The next floor was too quiet. The drudge stood like a statue, one of Ferret's henchmen no doubt having used a kill switch on it when they realized was happening.

Moss saw bodies littering the floor. The music had stopped, the rhythmic lights flashing to silence. Ferret lay dead in his chair. From behind the DJ booth, a man stepped out with a gloved hand cupped over Ynna's mouth and a pistol to her head.

He was young, a mere child, and looked terrified. Moss knew a wrong move could get her killed. He was aligned with the window such that a shot from Gibbs would hit Ynna as well. Moss figured the kid's glove had a transmission dampener so they could not communicate without speaking or she would have warned him. Moss squared his shoulders, aiming the pistol.

The boy looked at him with terror, but demanded, "Put it down."

"Your boss is dead, don't throw your life away for nothing," Moss pleaded.

"My boss has bosses, I'll be the man if I bring you assholes in," his voice cracked as he spoke.

"Put your weapon down and just walk out," Moss said, sliding his body to the side. Ynna shifted in tandem, and the kid readjusted, pointing his weapon at Moss. Ynna did not wait for the dance to continue so Gibbs could align his shot, quickly bustling from his one arm grip and pulling his other down over her shoulder. His arm cracked, and he screamed out as she pulled the pistol free. She wheeled and kicked him to the ground, pointing his gun at him.

He held up a hand. "Please, you're on camera anyway, killing me gets you nothing," he pleaded, already beginning to cry.

Ynna loomed over him. "But it will feel good."

"Momma, I'm sorry," he cried out into the ether.

Ynna lowered her weapon. "It's too ugly," she said, turning to Moss. "We're supposed to be the good guys."

Moss agreed, stepping forward and firing a non-lethal. Amidst all this carnage, he still liked to think of himself as good.

"Plus, Gibbs wouldn't like it," she added. "He's a delicate flower."

"Should see what he did to the guy downstairs," Moss said as they rushed toward the exit. They knew Carcer didn't care about this district, but a bloodbath might draw their attention. "How the hell did he get you?" Moss asked.

"One of these guys was a fucking ninja or something. Shot him as he roundhoused me in the face, but I was seeing stars long enough for that kid to grab me. You men are all the fucking same," she bristled. "Grazed my tit in the struggle and I swear he had a hardon."

"Yeah, we're all pretty gross," Moss agreed as they rushed down the now abandoned stairs.

"Issy ever talk to you about fucking a robo version of her?" Ynna asked.

Moss felt his face flush. "Gibbs told you?" he hollered in annoyance out on the street.

She wheeled on him with a broad smile and said, "He did!"

"Can't trust him for anything," Moss groused.

"Nope! So, did you?" she pressed, the side of her face red and likely to bruise badly. She was nearly skipping backward as they walked.

"No," Moss admitted, "but I think she knows."

"Oh, shit!" Ynna exclaimed, pushing Moss playfully on the shoulder before slinging her rifle over her back.

Gibbs came running over, red-faced and panting.

"You fucking told her?" Moss shouted.

"Told her what? Is now really the time?" Gibbs gasped, confused and seemingly worried.

"A time will come," Moss said ominously. "But we need to clear out."

"You guys get anything off the bodies? Weapons or money or anything?" Gibbs asked as they made their way down the few doors. The street was empty now, everyone cowering in their homes. The sound of gunplay was familiar to the people of the Burg, and they knew better than to get involved.

"We didn't loot them," Ynna said. "We mostly were trying to get out alive."

"Fine," Gibbs allowed. "But next time, try to get us some supplies. We're destitute out here."

"Hopefully, there won't be a next time," Moss said.

"There is always a next time," Ynna intoned.

CHAPTER 6

They stood before Powers, who was grinning with surprise.

"Where have you three been all my life?" he asked with excitement. "Efficiency like this, I could have taken over the whole neighborhood years ago!"

"We are good at some things," Moss allowed.

"Don't be so modest," he said. "You did in an hour what the idiots outside couldn't plan in a year. And I've been trying, I'll tell you that."

The adrenaline had worn off, and Moss was now too tired for this man's enthusiasm.

"You caught us at a desperate time is all," said Ynna modestly, but her pride showed through.

"Lucky for me," Powers said.

"One of them mentioned that Ferret had bosses who would be none too pleased," Moss led.

"No doubt, no doubt," Powers said. "But that is for me to sort out, and right now I am the power in this district, so I'm not scared of any retaliation."

"As for our reward?" Moss asked.

"You have it! And more!" Powers said chipperly. He seemed

like an athlete after winning a big game, and Moss knew now would be the time to get what they could.

"We need some supplies for our journey and what comes after," he said.

"I'll take you to my storeroom myself, and you can take whatever you need," Powers said graciously. "But they don't do runs at night, so tonight we celebrate, and in the morning, you'll be on your way."

"Thank you," Ynna said.

"It is truly my pleasure," Powers responded. "May I ask you one question, as we are but new friends here?"

"Certainly," Moss said, though he expected what the query might be.

"Who are you?"

"Well, as I mentioned—" Moss began, and Powers waved a dismissive hand.

"Not the fake names, I mean, who are you?" he pressed.

"Better if we don't say," Ynna nearly whispered, "for all of us."

"Understood," Powers winked. "Let us go to my restaurant and eat and drink in celebration. You may shop thereafter, and I will set you up in one of my apartments before your long trip. I presume it's better that I also don't ask the destination?"

"Correct," Moss said.

"So it is." Powers smiled, opening the door and leading them from the office. The thugs beyond looked on the three with a mixture of surprise, anger, and jealous respect. He turned to the bartender, "I'm walking away, clear the streets."

"I'll send a crew, but the streets are already clear, boss," the bartender explained.

"Of course, they are. Wonderful, just wonderful," he said, rubbing his hands together in excitement. He strode out on to the empty street and took a deep breath of heavy night air. Eyes watched from windows along the wall side of the street, but no one made a sound.

He spread his arms wide and strutted down the street with his eyes closed for a moment, the lights from the bar windows glistening off his head. The three walked behind him in silence, watching uncomfortably. A few Hoplites followed behind, looking threatening though there was no one to intimidate. Rickshaws and bicycles lay abandoned along the narrow space, their owners likely cowering inside the nearest building. Powers tripped in a pothole but steadied himself quickly.

"You know what I'm going to do?" he asked no one in particular as he pointed to the deteriorated road.

When no one spoke, Gibbs filled the silence, "What's that?"

"I'm going to give back," he announced with pride.

"How?" Gibbs said as it seemed no one else would.

"I'm happy you asked, little man," Powers said over his shoulder. "With that prick gone, I expect I will take all his business in the neighborhood and will become even richer than I already am—though I am already enormously wealthy. But unlike Ferret, I will give back to this place which has raised me."

"Raised you," Gibbs said, "don't you have a bit of an accent, or were you raised in a Russian corner of the city?"

Powers laughed. "It's a bit of both. I was born in Novosibirsk, but my mother wanted a better life—stop me if you've heard this one. She signed a contract and moved to the great BA City. As is always the case, she had not read the fine print, and she worked in a robotics lab for nearly no money and began borrowing from the company to feed me and my brothers. You know the con from here. The company offered her new contracts as a condition of the loan, and she quite actually died at her desk. And that's why I want to give back. The people here all suffer. They cannot afford to pay even for road upkeep. I can do these things for them."

"It will certainly ingratiate you to the people," Moss said, finding it interesting that he felt a kinship with this local gangster.

"I do it not for the love, but because it's the right thing to do. One should always help those who helped them," he stated.

"You're a good man," Ynna said, somewhat ironically.

"You seem a good lot, too," Powers told them.

"We try," Gibbs smiled. They reached the restaurant, the neon signs written in Russian.

"Called Katia's, after my mother," Powers informed them.

"That's nice," Ynna said.

"Yes, my brothers are the cooks here. Best stuffed cabbage in the city," he boasted.

"Can't say I've tried it," Moss admitted.

"If my friendship doesn't bring you back to here, the food will," he said, holding the door open for them. As they stepped in, it felt like a different world. Well-dressed men and women sat at red tableclothed tables with fine silver cutlery. The servers were dressed in elegant tuxedoes, bringing platters of food which steamed dramatically as they lifted cloches table-side. The walls were painted in a dull floral pattern and dim, round lights hung from the ceiling on gold chains, illuminating an emerald green floor.

"Sir James would love this place," Gibbs observed, and Ynna clicked her tongue. Powers noticed.

"A more elegant man, I have never met," Powers said, "and your friendship tells me much, though your secret is safe with me."

Gibbs flushed.

"I feel underdressed," Moss said, hoping to cut the tension.

"No friend of mine is ever underdressed," Powers told them, though the other diners looked upon them with judgment. Waiters pulled out the chairs so the four could sit, which they did uneasily. "I have a restaurant for people who live to eat, but I want to give to those who eat to live," he said, getting back to his previous point. He had a real pride about what he did.

"We can relate," Moss said.

"This I now know," Powers put simply. A moment later, a loaf of warm bread was set on the table with a dish of butter, rock salt glistening on top. Bowls of a red stew were placed before them, a white dollop of cream in the center.

"Eat, my friends," he said as he reached out and tore off some bread, crumbs scattering to the table. "People love to hate the ingredients created in labs, but I find, with the right cook, they can be better than the excruciatingly expensive real thing."

Moss grimaced but tried to hide it. He had spent his whole life eating lab-grown ingredients, and now that he had eaten the real thing, he didn't want to go back. But he dipped his spoon and found that Powers was correct.

"Delicious," Gibbs said between slurps.

"Thank you," Powers beamed. "I will tell my brothers."

"Please do," Gibbs said, soaking up the last of the broth with some bread. Glasses of clear liqueur were put on the table.

"Now, the night shall begin," Powers announced, gulping down a shot. The three followed suit, the vodka burning down Moss's throat. Powers spoke Russian to one of the waiters who quickly returned with a sedative pack for Ynna's face and a small medical bag. "You don't mind?" he asked Moss, who had all but forgotten about the injury to his head.

"Oh, yes, please. Thank you," Moss said, tilting his head and allowing the man to wipe his wound.

"Vasily was a doctor before coming to BA," Powers explained, though Moss hardly heard it, already warm with drink.

"On weekends, we set up station for locals to come and eat this food for free," Powers boasted.

"That's very kind," Gibbs said. Moss noted that his friend

was doing a good job keeping the man happy. Ynna was refilling her glass and pressing the compress to her face. She looked content, and at that moment, Moss was, too.

BY THE END of the meal, they were all well drunk and full. By the time the dessert pancakes arrived, they thought they could eat no more. After taking a single bite to not seem rude, Moss found himself finishing the entire plate. He slid the plate away with satisfaction.

"Thank you," Moss said.

"It was my pleasure. Sharing a meal with likeminded individuals such as yourselves is a treat for me," he said.

Ynna pointed a finger and slurred, "Plus, we killed your competition."

"And there is that," he responded with a broad smile. "He really was a piece of shit."

"Seemed like it," Ynna agreed.

"Must have hated you, strong woman such as you are," he snorted.

"We were warned, so Mo—Che did the talking," Ynna said, correcting herself too late to go unnoticed. Powers seemed neither surprised nor interested.

"Good plan, good thinking," Powers said. "The way he treated women... disgraceful. People in general, really. I had employees of his knocking down my door for a switch."

"That reminds me," Moss began, his tongue loose with booze. "I notice you hire bikers rather than drudges or your own local people."

"Ah," Powers said, "that is my genius. I have my own people, of that you should have no doubt, but the Hoplites were already a fixture in this neighborhood. Rather than fighting a war on two fronts, I befriended the bikers with the unicameral language of money. They are already angry and loyal and willing to do whatever is asked—the perfect fit for a man such as myself. Their leaders get a large kickback, and I get an army. Lose one, and another prospect shows up at my doorstep the following morning. And a person cannot be hacked."

"Like a drudge, you mean?" Gibbs clarified.

"Exactly," Powers said, turning to Ynna, "not that I need to tell you."

"Watching that, were you?" she asked.

"Naturally," he told them. None were surprised. "I will fall asleep to that video this very night."

"Gross," Ynna said, picking up on his implication, her filter all but gone. Having sat and enjoyed a meal after all that they had gone through, they had nothing left in the tank.

"Beautiful," he said dreamily. "Would you like to see some toys?"

"Yes," Moss said, standing. His robotic legs compensated for a wobbling mind.

"We have far to go?" Gibbs asked, sounding as if he feared he could not walk any distance without falling.

"Not my first day," Powers grinned. "Through the kitchen and down some stairs."

"Great," Ynna said, her hand gripping the back of her chair for balance.

"Follow this way," Powers said, his accent having grown thicker with every drink. He guided them to the kitchen where Gibbs stopped.

"Great meal," he told the cooks, who looked quizzically to Powers. He repeated in Russian, and they all smiled and nodded. Powers opened a walk-in refrigerator and moved beyond the vats which glowed blue. Powers waved a hand, and the rear wall of the container slid open.

"Another secret door," Moss said with a chuckle.

"This city is all secret doors," Powers noted seriously and led them down a flight of stairs to a long room with metal racks lining both walls. The fluorescent lights were painful, and he and Gibbs found themselves shielding their eyes. Ynna's adjusted automatically, and Powers had kept his glasses on even through dinner.

"Whatever you desire," Powers said with a sweeping motion before picking up bags from a nearby shelf and handing them out. Moss had been in rooms like this before but never with a blank check. They all grinned. Ynna made straight for a rack of designer clothes and unopened shoeboxes.

"Really?" Gibbs asked her incredulously.

"I'm wearing fucking lost and found," Ynna shot back, running her fingers over the fine fabrics.

"Still just a rich kid," Moss piled on.

"Eat shit, Moss," she chided absently, lost in the clothes.

Moss walked down the long corridor to a line of Kingfisher pistols. He had become accustomed to the feel of them and didn't want to have to adjust too much. Moss saw a sleek black pistol with enhanced battery, auto-targeting and four settings where his had two: lethal and non. He picked it up and noted the weight. It was much heavier and of sturdier build.

"Never seen this style before," Moss told Powers as he watched them shop.

"It's not on the market yet," he said with a clever smile. "Fell off truck, as they say."

"And I can just—" Moss began.

"Take it. As I said, whatever you desire," Powers said, enjoying their excitement. Moss passed Gibbs who was unfolding and retracting long rifles. Moss began to look at Dermidos bodysuits, each with its own purpose. At the end of the line were several he did not recognize, and he beckoned Powers to join him.

"You have quite an eye," Powers said. "It's a good thing I like you."

Moss looked at him anxiously. "Yeah?"

"This is made from off-world compounds, tech which has hardly yet reached our planet. Has dial here by the wrist and can alter to fit your needs. Camera blindness, thermal adjustment, naked eye cloaking, anything you could dream of, truthfully," he explained.

"And we can just take three?" Moss asked sheepishly.

"These, I may want back," Powers said.

"We could compensate you when all is said and done," Ynna offered, walking over and stuffing a duffle bag full of clothes.

"Money, I have," he reminded them. "This is much more difficult to come by. Intercepting trade routes among the stars is not so easily done."

"I'll bet," Gibbs said, now paying attention, too.

"But for now, you may take them," he said, and the three snatched them off the rack. Ynna backtracked, and Moss saw her pause before a row of weaponry. She pulled a handheld beam weapon and admired it with a solemn smile. Moss recognized the gun instantly as the line laser which Burn had carried. Though slow to recharge, the weapon fired a devastating flat beam which made short work of man and machine alike. Powers gave her a calculating look but said nothing.

"He'd like that," Moss said.

"I think so," Ynna agreed, and silence hung in the air.

"It's been a long night for you and an even longer day awaits, shall I take you to the apartment?" Powers asked.

"One last thing," Moss said, and looked to Ynna, who nodded. "Do you have any Carcer attire?"

CHAPTER 7

The apartment to which Powers brought them was a shrine to opulence—styled in sleek black and polished chrome, screens on every wall with every item controlled electronically.

"Hexes have nothing on this," Gibbs said and turned in the direction of the open kitchen, "Wine, please." A long, slender countertop made a noise from beneath before opening, an open bottle of wine and three glasses rising out. He grinned with excitement and hustled over, pouring the dark liquid. He turned, a sadness in his eyes. Moss knew what he was thinking. "I know it's wrong for us to live like this while our friends are, well, wherever they are, but we can't leave until the morning, and we earned this."

"True," Ynna agreed, grabbing a glass. "There is nothing we can do for them tonight, and we have been through a lot ourselves."

"We have," Moss agreed, picking up a glass. "What do you think is happening to them now?"

"Being processed," Ynna said, taking a sip. "The torture probably won't begin until they get them to the city."

"Really?" Gibbs asked in astonishment.

"Carcer won, they have them now and probably won't be in a rush. The assholes will take our friends to a controlled environment so they can do what they want, how they want."

"Won't they want to know," Moss trailed off.

"You're not that important to them now. Gotta figure they think you're just some bub out on his own. They probably figure they expect to fish your corpse out of some gutter in a few days," she said, looking at her glass and adding, "This is really good."

"How long before they get to the city?" Moss asked.

"Probably a day. Those guys will stay strong, though, until we can get there. It'll be toughest on Judy. Carcer sees things in black and white—biotch augmented and not. Male and female. They won't respect Judy's wishes," Ynna said, not looking up and tracing the rim of her glass with her fingertip.

"This fucking world," Moss snarled.

"Judy's a tough nut though," Ynna said. "But seriously, we can't dwell on this shit all night."

"Telling us, or yourself?" Gibbs asked. She looked up, determined to shake the sadness. Moss took a sip of the wine, the flavor coating his tongue. He took a second sip.

"Oh," he exclaimed. "This is something. The rich know how to live."

Ynna looked up at him with amusement. "Think you're on the wrong side of this thing?"

"Maybe," Moss replied in exaggerated consideration. Gibbs and Ynna smiled. "I'm just saying I would oppress a lot of people for wine like this."

"Then you are halfway there!" Ynna said with a laugh.

Silence followed a moment.

Gibbs turned to Ynna. "Can I ask you something I've been dying to know?"

"No, I won't sleep with you," she answered with a sly smirk. Gibbs turned a bright crimson.

"That wasn't it," he stuttered, taking a gulp of wine and wincing. "Your name?"

"What about it?" she asked, playing dumb.

"It's unusual," Gibbs said, so straight-faced that Moss couldn't help but laugh.

"As opposed to Moss," Ynna said, pointing a finger.

"At least Moss is a word," Moss defended. "When I first heard your name, I assumed it was spelled e-e-n-a."

"That makes no sense," Ynna said, though the amusement was obvious.

"Because y-n-n-a is pretty normal?" Gibbs cried out.

"Fine, fine, I give up," Ynna said, raising a hand. "When I was little, my baby brother couldn't pronounce my name, so I started going by Ynna. Happy?"

"You have a brother?" Moss and Gibbs asked in unison.

She had expected this question, and her face dropped. "He died when I was very little."

"Sorry," Moss said.

"How?" Gibbs asked. "I mean, sorry, too, but how? I didn't think the rich had much in the way of mortality."

"Fell down a staircase. Not much anyone can do for a broken neck," Ynna said. "It was a long time ago, and I hardly remember it now."

Not knowing what else to say, Moss repeated, "Sorry."

"It is what it is," Ynna said. "Now Gibbs, what's with you and the old-time stuff?"

Moss groaned, and Gibbs punched him lightly. "I think I just like the simpler time. Movies filmed with real actors on real sets. Everything now is so produced. Can't tell the difference between the real and the digital. So loud and flashy. It's exhausting."

"What is your favorite type of old movie?" she asked, sounding genuinely interested.

"Westerns," Gibbs said without having to think about it. Moss had always watched as his friend forced uninterested people to listen to him wax on about the things he loved, and he was happy that for once in his life, someone actually wanted to know. "The sweeping vistas, long, slow shots of the country. Unequivocal good and evil. The fight between man and nature before man always won. There is a simple beauty to the genre which attracts me."

"I can see that," Ynna said with a smile. "Will you play one for us tonight?"

Gibbs looked as though he was going to vibrate off the earth, he was so excited, "I will!"

"While we are being honest, Moss, what do you remember of your parents?" Ynna asked.

"Not sure I'm in the mood for truth or dare," Moss said quietly.

"Oh please, if this were truth or dare, Gibbs would have me streaking down the hallways as quick as he could," Ynna chided.

"That is true," Gibbs affirmed with a laugh.

"I just want to know," Ynna said. "I knew your dad as a very different man than the one I'm sure you did."

"That's what's so weird," Moss began. "I didn't know the man who wanted to take down ThutoCo, the man who helped form this group. I knew a simple, hardworking version who was just dad, you know? He was just the guy who wanted to tuck me in at night. The person who would sit and watch the tigers with me for hours because he knew I loved it.

"When you first showed up at my door, talking of big plans, I had no idea what that could be about. It was nothing the people I knew as my parents had even prepared me for."

"It showed," Ynna said.

"I know it," Moss said with a little smile. "I have flashes of memories. The moment so scary that the brain wipe couldn't fully erase it. The lights coming through the door, my father calling out to me as he was dragged away. It's like remembering a dream. A thought so vague that I can't quite get my hands around it. I don't know if this makes any sense?"

"It does," Ynna assured him.

"And my grandmother... the woman I didn't recognize being beaten by Ninety-Nine, she was a kind woman who loved to give me little trinkets when she came to visit. I never knew she was a warrior—a tough woman who made those around her stronger. A woman whose death could crush the soul of the toughest man I ever met," he said, thinking about Burn getting drunk night after night in Jo's saloon.

"I ever tell you how I met Sandra?" Ynna asked.

"No," Moss said.

"It was the early days of all this. She and Burn were only beginning to bring people together. Grimy had brought me in, and Burn was beginning to show me that I could use my skills with purpose. But the whole thing felt like a boy's club, even with just the two of them. A few days in, Sandra showed up, back from some mission. She was bloody and bedraggled and pissed. She took one look at me and just said, "What the fuck is this?"

"I had thought I was such a badass but had recently gotten my ass kicked and her words cut through me like a shot. Made me question if I had any value at all or if I was just the spoiled rich kid everyone assumed I was. Burn just told me to give her time, wait it out, but I was butthurt and proud and stormed out.

"Back on the street, I was trying to run a scam on a wealthy businessman, but I was pissed and failing miserably. He was about to call Carcer on me. The gig was up, but Sandra walked over and hollered at me like I was her daughter. The businessman thought I was just some runaway and backed off, thinking I was gonna get worse from my mom than anything Carcer could do to me.

"Sandra looked on me with pity and told me I would need to toughen up if I wanted to run with them. I know now that Burn sent her after me, but at the time, it was what I needed to hear. She began training me, too. Her and Burn taking turns showing me the ropes. Made me the woman I am now. I'll never forget how she saved my ass when she still thought I was just some stray."

"I want to know that woman," Moss said.

Ynna smiled softly at him. "You will."

"I wish I was so confident," Moss replied.

Gibbs gave a weak smile. "Hope is what we have."

Moss looked at Ynna. "Ever been outside the city?"

"Not really, and I'm guessing you haven't either?" she said, and though Moss noted the evasive answer, he let it go.

"Sorta," Moss answered. "I mean, never physically."

"What does that mean?" she asked, never having investigated his life in the Burb too deeply.

"My job was to control a drudge who worked outside the walls," he stated.

"Right, the ones who were supposed to be uploaded with your personalities and replace you," she said.

"Exactly. My days were spent seeing the world through his camera, out in the fields. Mostly crops and solar panels. I would repair the machinery," he explained.

"Tell her your drudge's name," Gibbs smirked.

"You're the fucking worst!" Moss stated. "You know I regret it! Plus, you told her about the Relief Aide!"

"I had to tell someone, and there are so few people to gossip to anymore," Gibbs defended, though he was obviously amused.

"Or you could just not gossip," Ynna put in, "not that it wasn't hilarious to find out."

"I dislike both of you." Moss took another gulp of wine as the others giggled.

"Its name was MOSS II!" Gibbs shrieked with glee.

At that, Ynna let out a hearty laugh and quickly covered her mouth with her hands. "Very clever."

"Right?" Gibbs guffawed. Moss tried to turn the page.

"So, while I have never been out in the world, I have worked in it remotely," he said, but the other two were having far too much fun.

"We should get a cat and call it Moss III," Ynna joked.

"What about Moss Junior?" Gibbs piled on.

"Lord Mossington the Twelfth." Ynna snorted through laughter.

"Mossamillion Mosslebottom," Gibbs shouted. The room fell silent as the two attempted to concoct more names.

"Mossy something," Ynna said, but the moment had passed.

"Are you two quite done?" Moss said.

"Where did your name even come from? I'm shocked I never thought to ask," Gibbs said.

"No idea," Moss said, "I never thought to ask either."

"I know," Ynna revealed, instantly gaining their full attention.

"I'm getting sick of realizing how much more you know about my family than I do," Moss said, and it was true.

"The first time I ever heard about you, I asked your dad where that name came from," she told them.

"And you didn't think to tell me when I asked about yours?" he shot.

"Assumed you knew," she said innocently.

"Let's have it," Moss said, making a beckoning gesture with his hand.

"He said it was a joke. Your grandmother always said she was a rolling stone, but she wanted security and stability for her family—before realizing what ThutoCo actually was," she said.

"Oh," Moss said, thinking about his father.

"What?" Gibbs asked.

"A rolling stone gathers no moss," he told his friend. "Dad loved expressions and turn of phrases like that. So, if I were the thing which held our family in place, I would be Moss."

"He really did love those things," Ynna agreed. "He would always say, 'I need that like—'"

"A moose needs a hat rack," Moss finished with a groan.

Ynna laughed. "Right."

"Is now the time where you tell us you really want to see a moose?" Gibbs asked.

"Yes," Moss said plainly. "You want to know what the most striking thing about the outside is, Ynna?" She nodded, leaning forward on the countertop. "Bird calls."

"What?" Ynna said, genuinely perplexed.

"The trilling of birds. You never hear it in the Burb or the city, but out in the fields, it's a constant sound. The drudges are programmed to filter it out, but a friend of mine—"

"Issy?" Gibbs interrupted.

"No," Moss said.

"Ricky?" Gibbs pressed.

"No, a friend from engineering, will you let me finish?" Moss groused, and Gibbs fell silent. "A friend told me that if you turn off the filter, one could hear the sound of the wild. It is wonderful."

"It's just I didn't really think you had friends other than us," Gibbs put in.

"Sounds great," Ynna rescued the moment.

"To be fair, there are birds in the city, too," Gibbs said.

"Yeah, pigeons, falcons, and vultures. It's not the same

thing," Moss said, tiring of his friend. "Should we watch a western now?"

The three plodded over to the couch, Ynna bringing over the wine bottle by one finger stuck in the top. The couch automatically shifted under their weight, extending footrests under their legs.

"This is the most comfortable couch in the world," Gibbs said as he put on the movie.

PART II

CHAPTER 8

A soft chime rang in the apartment as the autoshade dissolved off the windows, allowing in the light of day. Moss's whole body ached, and his head pounded. He licked his dry lips, the taste of stale wine nauseating in his mouth. The chime rang a second time, and he saw Ynna stride over to the door, fully dressed for the day ahead, her hair shimmering yellow now.

"Morning, sunshine," Gibbs said, stepping into view. He handed Moss a pill and a glass of water. "Seemed so tired, we let you sleep a little longer."

"What time is it?" Moss asked, throwing the pill in his mouth and slurping at the water before realizing it was vodka and gagging. Gibbs chuckled.

"Just let the pill do its thing, you'll be right as rain in a minute," he said. "The alcohol gets it working faster."

"You could have warned me," Moss sputtered, the liquid leaking from the corners of his mouth.

Gibbs smiled. "That would have been way less funny." Moss looked him over. He had the bodysuit on under clean gray jeans which hugged his legs and a shirt with specifically tailored tears.

A new, muted, black leather jacket fit snugly on his frame. He was freshly shaven, having given up on the wispy mustache he normally sported, and his orange hair was spiked up.

"She did good," Moss observed hoarsely, thinking that his friend really did look better dressed like this than in his usual, baggy attire.

"You think? I like it," he said with pride, pulling on the collars of the jacket.

"She get me anything?" Moss asked, looking to Ynna who was speaking to Powers at the door.

"No," Gibbs said sadly, "she said your style suits you."

"Oh, how nice," he said, sitting up painfully. The new Kingfisher had been pressing into his side overnight, the digifoam unable to contour to the awkward shape. The drug was already working, and his hangover was fading quickly. "I have time to shower?"

"Think so, and I made breakfast for you—bacon and eggs with orange juice," Gibbs said.

"You cooked?" Moss exclaimed.

"The kitchen helped," Gibbs admitted.

"And coffee might suit me better," Moss stood slowly and made his way to the bathroom, the pain he had been feeling quickly replaced by a singular pressure on his bladder.

AFTER RELUCTANTLY FORCING himself from the shower, Moss emerged into the main room of the apartment to find his plate in a warming nook. He pulled it and joined the three at the table.

"Now we are all here, I tell you the plan," Powers said, Moss forking the food in as he listened. "I have packed some provisions for you at the specifications of your transporter. She will take you as far as the first town, but from there you will need to make further arrangements for the next leg of your journey. The world is strictly patrolled and unsafe for people, so the trip will be perilous. If you have any remaining business in the city, I would take care of it in the next short while."

"The networks in here are secure?" Moss asked, suspecting he knew the answer.

"No more secure networks will you find anywhere," Powers affirmed.

"Good." Moss stood, his plate already clean of food. "I want to make a call."

"Ooh," Gibbs and Ynna called out like teenagers.

"You have some time," Powers said. "There are vidphones in the bedrooms, too."

"Thanks," Moss said, heading straight for a room and closing the door. He pulled the scrap of paper with Issy's routing number scrawled on it and input the information. A ringing tone emitted from the black screen and Moss worried that she wouldn't be there to answer. Her father, Vihaan's face appeared, filling the screen.

"Hello, young Moss. It's been too long," he said. "How are you?"

"Well, thank you," Moss said, his voice formally stilted.

"That is good to hear," he replied. "I presume it is my daughter to whom you wish to speak?"

"It is, not that it isn't nice to speak with you as well," Moss said.

"You are, as always, too kind," Vihaan said, turning his head and shouting, "Issy, call for you! Nice to see you, Moss."

"You too. I hope to visit soon," Moss told him.

"That would please me," Vihaan said and stood, exiting the frame. Moss stared at the blank yellow wall at which the camera pointed, his heart racing. He had spoken to Issy as often as he could, but it never felt safe, and it was still awkward. They had both been through so much. Issy appeared in the frame, her hair fluttering as she sat.

She smiled. "You look rough."

"A lot has happened," Moss said.

"With you, that's never a good thing," she replied.

"It isn't," Moss said gravely. "I'm going to be leaving for a while and just wanted to say bye in case," he said, dropping his head.

"Oh," was all she said, and the silence held. Moss didn't know what he could say, what he even wanted to say, and he sensed she felt the same. "I suppose I don't want to know?" she asked eventually.

"Better if you don't," he said.

"Well, I guess, good luck," she said, looking into the camera.

"Thanks," he said and added, "I'd like to come see you when I get back."

She looked away. "I'm not sure I'm ready. You know I want to see you, but I'm just," she trailed off.

"When you're ready then," he said. He had said that line so many times. He understood her feelings logically, but his heart called out for her. He missed seeing her. Just being around her made him feel happy. He had told her so. She had said she had felt the same, but things had also changed. He knew it, much as he didn't want it to be true.

"You'll call again when it's all over?" she asked, indicating an end to the conversation.

"I will," he promised.

"Good, I really like hearing from you," she said, having used those words many times before, as well. He felt as though they were in this repeating loop from which they didn't know how to break free.

"I like it, too," he said. "Bye, Issy."

"Goodbye, Moss," she replied, and the screen blanked. He

felt empty. He wasn't sure what he had expected from that call, but he knew that wasn't what he wanted. He ran his fingers through his damp hair and sighed.

"I'M READY," he announced to the room sullenly, and no one asked how the call went.

"Good," Powers replied, standing. Gibbs handed Moss a metal cup of coffee.

"For the road," his friend told him.

"Thank you for everything," Moss said to Powers, who smiled his gold smile.

"New friends are a rare treat. I'm glad to have met you, even if it's under unusual circumstances," he said, adjusting a thin, squared tie. With vest and suit jacket, he looked even larger than he had the night before.

"Unusual is one word for it," Ynna joked.

"Whatever the word, I'm happy to know you all," he said, shaking their hands one by one. "I'll still want those suits back," he reminded them with a wink, guiding them from the apartment. They descended the stairs, leaving through the same convenience store through which they had entered, the same tired old woman glancing up at them for a brief moment before returning to a blaring screen.

Stepping out onto the street, Moss realized it was later than he had expected, close to midday. The street had returned to its bustle, people milling about and many more hanging out the windows of the wall-side apartments. Food sizzled in carts, projected models shifted and posed while children darted about, playing and asking for handouts.

They approached a nondescript apartment door, and Powers gave a specific knock upon the door, and a chain clattered on the other side. The sheet metal door opened slowly.

"Here for Martha," Powers said.

"I know it, send them in," a voice said. It sounded to Moss like a child.

Powers turned to them, handing Moss a bag. "I hope to see you again."

"Us, too," Moss replied, "for many reasons."

Powers nodded and strode away, people shifting respectfully from his path.

"In, in," the voice from inside whispered again, cracking the door a little further. They squeezed into the dark room, unable to see anything when the kid closed the door, having to give it a little kick to secure it.

"I take you to mother," the kid said, and kid he was. As Moss's eyes became able to see, he realized it was a boy of about ten. He was energetic, moving with the excitement of youth and was dressed in shabby, tattered clothes, his shirt an obvious free giveaway from a cosmetics company. He had olive skin and big, brown eyes which caught the slight light streaming through breaks in the metal.

He guided them rapidly down some pressed earth stairs to a nearly empty room with a dirt floor and artistic posters of various cities peeling from the walls.

"Sit, sit," the boy said, gesturing hurriedly to a bench which consisted of little more than two-by-fours on cinderblocks. They sat.

Glancing around the dingy, spartan room, Gibbs observed, "This is ominous."

"You expected something fancy?" Ynna chided.

"After last night, I've become accustomed to a certain life-style," he joked with a nervous smile.

"Pretty sure that's the last of *that* lifestyle we are likely to see," Moss said.

"It's about to get a lot grimmer from here," Ynna added.

The room rumbled, the entire back wall grinding slowly open. A woman entered, calculating eyes under a low brow line. Her jet-black hair was graying at the base and pulled into a tight bun.

"Hello," she said with a slight accent.

Moss was struck once again by how different the Burbs were from the city. Where he had grown up, everyone spoke with the same general accent, like the people on television. Vihaan was one of the only people he had known who had an accent. But out in the city, people seemed to be from everywhere.

"Good morning," Moss said.

"Not quite." She smiled. "I'm Martha."

They introduced themselves, continuing to use their false names just to be on the safe side. She appraised them quickly. "Have any of you been outside the city?"

"No," they all answered.

"Okay," she said, "follow me. You brought water? This is to be a long walk."

"We did," Ynna said, turning to Moss. "Powers packed it with some other things for us."

"Good," Moss said, looking at the mug of coffee in his hands.

They followed down the dug tunnel, the smell of sweat and dirt filling their nostrils. Rotting wood beams kept the tunnel from collapsing in, and lights were strung down its length. It twisted and stretched, and Moss had no idea how long it could go. Perspiration began to build on all of them, their breathing becoming labored as the tight space stretched on.

Gibbs huffed. "I didn't realize we were getting right into it."

"Me neither," Ynna agreed.

"This is just the first leg. We are in this tunnel a long time. Sometimes it helps to play games, have any of you tried eye-spy?" Martha asked with a smile over her shoulder.

"No," Moss said.

"It was a joke," Ynna chuckled.

"It was an attempt at humor," Martha affirmed.

They trudged forward for another hour in silence. The air turned thick and unbreathable.

"How much further," Gibbs panted, red and exhausted, running hands along the walls.

"A bit," Martha told him, handing back a bottle of water she kept in a leather tool belt. He gulped at it before Martha grabbed it back in a sputtering spray. "Not too much," she warned.

"Right," Gibbs said, drenched. He rubbed his face, dirt from the wall wiping onto his skin.

"What awaits us?" Moss inquired.

"Change into protective gear, get into our transport," she told them clearly. A thin line of perspiration dotted her hairline, but she didn't seem tired.

"Where will we go?" Ynna asked.

"A town very different from where you come," Martha informed them. "From there, I will introduce you around, and you can buy a ride further along. Where is your destination?"

"Carcer City," Ynna said, turning back to add, "no reason to hide it now."

Martha's face grew grim. "There are some who will take you, but that is, how you say, risky? High risk."

"We know," Ynna said.

"I will introduce you to a reputable man," Martha offered.

"Thank you," Ynna said.

"You," Martha said, gesturing to Ynna, "will be unpopular."

Ynna looked concerned, asking, "Why?"

"Obvious biotech augments. Not popular among the scubas," Martha informed them. "People outside are simpler. It's a hard life, makes hard folk."

Moss's jaw dropped. He should have known. It was obvious, but he hadn't thought of it. "Scubas?" he hissed derisively.

"Yes," Martha put plainly. Moss snorted, and Gibbs joined in. Ynna looked at them with confusion. "What?"

"They were the bane of my existence in my old job. Running raids on our facilities, stealing tech, destroying, pilfering supplies, anything you could think of, they did it," Moss complained.

"That's a good thing," Ynna reminded him.

"Sure, yeah, I know. I mean, I see that now, but you have to understand... It's just, they were so annoying and every morning Two would tell me about some damage and I know it's a good thing, and ThutoCo is evil, but it was still annoying," Moss sputtered, thinking about the Scubas.

"Well, get over it, they're the good guys now," Ynna said.

"Even still," Moss said, annoyed even though he knew she was right.

"Good guys may be a bit of an overstating," Martha said.

"You seem to have no love for the people you work with," Gibbs observed.

"The outsiders live a very different life, as I've said. They look on us with... scorn," she stated.

"I'm getting nervous," Gibbs said.

"Correct," Martha affirmed as they finally reached a wooden door which she opened with a key. "Hopefully, we won't need," she told them, pointing to oxygen tanks. "Please," she gestured, and they all began to strap the tanks to their backs. "Purifiers are in the car, but if we break down, we use this."

"You break down a lot?" Gibbs worried.

"No, but good to be safe," she said. The lights were strung around many wooden beams to provide a soft light. A garage door lay on the other side of the room, built into the earth.

Martha pushed the base of the door down with her foot before sliding it up and open.

A bunker was set into the earth on the other side. Three walls of concrete and an automated door surrounded a van hovering over a charging pad. Satellites and cloaking devices adorned the top of the vehicle. The tanks were heavy and shifted awkwardly on their tired bodies as she slid open a side door, and they clambered in. The seats had been modified, cut away in large pieces to allow for the tanks.

"The bacteria is airborne?" Gibbs clarified as Martha pulled herself into the front seat and turned on the computers.

"The disease seems to be. Outsider researchers study it but is high risk. From what they have said, a spore kills the host and uses the brain to carry it," she explained.

Gibbs seemed excited. "Wait, you're saying it kills the person and uses their body to infect others? Is a headshot all that kills them?"

"You have a strange attitude about this," Martha pointed out. "Do you know little of the disease?"

"We know almost nothing," Moss told her, cutting Gibbs off. "We know it killed a huge amount of the world's population but little else."

"We know not much more: spore, fungi, bacteria, all these words are used, but actual *information* is uncommon," she said, opening the garage door and driving forward into another where the vehicle was washed. Aids rolled down the windows as a final door opened to let in the afternoon light. "We steal the liquid from the misters to coat our cars. Dangerous work. Part of why this endeavor costs so much."

"Everything about your work sounds dangerous," Moss said, settling into his seat.

"Accurate observation," Martha agreed, pulling on well-worn

driving gloves and carefully pulling the van out into the wide world.

Gibbs and Ynna had their faces nearly pressed against the windows and Moss glanced out of the rear. From the outside, the massive doors were covered in brown concrete to give it the appearance of dirt, and the entire structure was covered over with earth.

As they pulled away, Moss could see the fields of massive spires spraying the mist which kept the city safe from infection. The city loomed behind, tall buildings glinting in the sun. The van picked up speed, moving quickly over the desolate land. Soon enough, the fields of prophet root began, stretching on interminably in every direction. In some odd way, it felt like home.

Before long, the subtle bouncing and endless sameness got the better of him, and he fell asleep.

CHAPTER 9

Moss opened his eyes as the van slowed to a halt. Ynna and Gibbs were both asleep, mouths open. A little drool leaked from Gibbs' mouth. It was dark but did not seem to be night, and Moss looked beyond his friend to see dense forest all around them, tall trees reaching into the sky to blot out the sun. He looked ahead to see why they stopped and his heart began to race.

In the road, he saw a massive brown creature with a long snout and thick fur coat. Two smaller versions bound around, tussling and tumbling with one another. "Grizzly bears," Martha whispered.

"There are still animals out here?" Moss asked, astonished. He had sometimes seen tracks and droppings from animals as he sped around on MOSS II's bike, but he had never seen any.

"In the forests, yes," she told him with a broad smile. "Many forests were planted with genetically altered trees that grow much faster than normal, but some ancient spots were left alone."

"Why?" Moss asked.

"When the companies were clear-cutting the world, many

protested. They set aside some wild places as appeasement. They could, no doubt, get away with tearing these places down now as there is nobody left who remembers, but they do not. Or have not yet, rather."

Moss snorted. "Probably just so the managers can tell themselves they haven't taken over the whole planet."

"Probably," Martha agreed. They sat in silence as the animals played in the road a little while longer before disappearing into the brush.

"Incredible," Moss said, his eyes wide and heart full.

Ynna grunted and looked around. "We here?"

"No, a little while longer," Martha said.

"Ynna, you just missed a bear," Moss told her enthusiastically.

"I've been to a zoo," she said with a dismissive wave of her hand before closing her eyes again.

"You see things like this a lot?" Moss asked, trying to lean forward to talk but restricted by the heavy tank.

"Sometimes," Martha said. "Many animals we thought lost reappeared when man fled to the city."

"Good," Moss said. He was heartened to know that some life had persisted. "The bacteria doesn't affect them?"

"No, the disease impacts humans only," she informed him.

"Good, these animals deserve this place more than we do," Moss found himself saying. Martha snickered.

"You will get on well with the outsiders, I think," she said.

"We'll see," Moss said as the van accelerated forward.

THEY DROVE A WHILE LONGER, Moss watching out the window for more signs of life but seeing none. Eventually, as they crested a hill, he saw it—a large glass dome surrounded by forests.

"What?" he exclaimed, and the other two woke up. Gibbs rubbed his eyes and wiped his face. Ynna simply stared.

"Not what you expected?" Martha grinned.

"How?" Moss asked. "Isn't this all company land?"

"Ah, yes," Martha nodded.

"So how can a place like this exist? Doesn't ThutoCo look for them?" Moss said, nonplussed.

"They do, and yet many places like this exist," she said. Moss wanted more than cagy answers.

"How?" he pressed, and she laughed.

"Breakers work 'round the clock to keep this place hidden from all scans and aerial images. Also, ThutoCo doesn't actually work that hard to find them," she said. Moss fumed. He had always been told the company was doing everything they could to find and eradicate the scubas. Intellectually, he knew they were an evil corporation who had planned on killing their employees, but it still needled him that they had lied about their efforts.

"Cost of doing business," Gibbs chuckled, shaking his head.

"Your guess is as good as mine," Martha replied as they descended into the little valley. The dome grew larger, reflecting the sunset magnificently. The road led to another anteroom for vehicles and Martha gave a little wave through the windshield to a guard in a tower. The tower connected to the dome at the base and was surrounded by windows, so the guard up top didn't have to wear a respirator. As they pulled closer, Moss could see the seams in the dome. He was amazed that not only did it exist undetected, but even that it had been built.

"Where did they get the supplies to build something like this?" Gibbs asked, seeming to read Moss's mind.

"Nobody now alive remembers," Martha said.

"She's not a fucking tour guide," Ynna chided.

"I am happy to try and answer questions. I just don't know

many things," Martha said as the car pulled through the open doors which closed behind them. The van was once again soaked with foam, but this time it was rinsed off with streams of water. "You may leave your tanks," she told them, and they hurried to pull the straps from their bodies.

"Happy we didn't need them," Gibbs said.

"Yes, very lucky," Martha agreed. "I will make introductions, but you will then be on your own."

"Thank you," Moss said as they all moved stiffly from the side door. A door opened at the front of the room, and a young woman entered. She was short and gaunt with long dirty blond dreadlocks and thin wool clothes. She smelled of sweat and body odor. She scanned them dubiously.

"What have you brought, Martha?" the young woman asked in an authoritative tone, narrowing her eyes at Ynna.

"City folk. On their way to C City. Won't trouble you for long," Martha answered. She turned to the three and said, "This is Princess Petal."

"Princess?" Ynna exclaimed.

"Way to make nice," Gibbs mocked under his breath.

"Yes, Princess. My father is the king here," Petal said, her voice echoing in the small room. "One of my roles here is to show visitors around, but if you cannot respect our laws or customs then perhaps you wish to go back to the city?"

"No, no," Moss said quickly. "We are pleased to make your acquaintance and would love a tour of your fine town."

Petal laughed at him. "You're getting the hang of it."

"I have business in town. If you'll excuse me," Martha said and hurried from the room, leaving them with the unfriendly princess.

"You go to Carcer City from here? Looking to turn yourselves in?" Petal smirked.

Moss smiled, and with an overly friendly tone said, "Something like that."

"And who, may I ask, are you?" she asked.

"Moss, Gibbs and Ynna," Moss told her, done with the fake names.

"Ynna is an unusual name," Petal observed with an unsubtle hint of condescension.

Ynna seethed. "I know."

"Shall I show you around?" Petal asked, seemingly pleased to have gotten under Ynna's skin.

"Yes, please," Moss ingratiated.

As they stepped from the final door out into the town, the heat hit them like a blast.

"Whoa," Gibbs said, wasting no time in pulling off his jacket. Moss followed suit, but Ynna simply pulled her sleeve down further to try and cover her metal hand.

"Yes, it is warm," Petal said with a smirk. "City dwellers take some time adjusting."

Moss looked up, seeing that there were vents built into the dome. "Would running the AC spread the disease?" he asked.

"No," she told them, but did not continue to speak, leaving them with the sense that she did not wish to say anything more.

The town was little more than a dirt thoroughfare with wooden structures on either side, reminding Moss of the movie they had watched the night before. Beyond the buildings were huts and tents with supplies. The road terminated at a large castle made of wood which towered over the town. Next to it was a church with a globe set atop the steeple. The people of the town seemed utterly disinterested in the visitors, giving them hardly a glance. They were all thin, tanned and weathered, wearing light and loose clothing in the heat.

"Here," Petal said with a gesture to a two-story building, "is the inn. I'll imagine you'll want to stop by there when we are done. Next door is the saloon where they have drinks, meals, and nightly performances. Next to that is the general store and a doctor's office just beyond. The rest of the buildings are homes or businesses which you don't need to trouble yourself with."

"Nice place," Gibbs said, wiping the sweat from his brow.

"How much is the inn per night?" Moss asked idly, and Petal laughed.

"Always about money with you city people. We don't traffic in that nonsense. Currency based economies make slaves of citizens. We barter here," Petal said.

Moss felt like a child the teacher had publicly mocked. "Oh."

"Powers gave us some stuff," Ynna whispered to him.

"How do you select leaders?" Gibbs asked. "Was your father elected as king?"

"No," Petal snapped. "He was trained to be king by his father and is doing the same for me. The royal family trains their children in the ways of just governance, and we rule the people with kindness. You people elect corrupt idiots to 'serve you' when they really serve whoever paid for them to win the election. Then you act shocked when they serve only the rich."

"We have no illusions about our puppet government," Moss said, and Petal smiled for the first time since they had met her.

"Then you are smarter than most," she said as they approached the end of the street. "Here is the church of Tellus, God of the Earth. We faithfully serve him, and he repays us with the bounty of the world."

As they passed, they saw several people in long frocks rubbing dirt on two naked men. They were chanting in a language Moss did not know. The men had their arms outstretched as the others pulled globs of wet mud from a trough at the base of the church.

They didn't need to ask for Petal to say, "These men have just completed a shift being corrupted by technology. They must be purified in the eyes of the father before returning to society."

"They are the ones who work the tech to keep you hidden?" Gibbs clarified.

"Yes," Princess Petal said, and their attention turned as the heavy door to the castle opened. A large man in a loincloth stepped out, flanked by two women holding guns in gloved hands. "Ah, here is my father, King Daffodil," Petal said with a sweeping gesture. He ambled down the steps, an amiable grin under a full gray beard. He was thin like his daughter but had a large gut which pushed down on the slight fabric.

"Greetings visitors," he said, opening his arms wide. "Welcome to my kingdom."

"It's an honor," Moss said up to him.

"Wonderful," he said happily, clapping his hands. "I presume my daughter has treated you well?"

"She has," Gibbs put in as the guards shifted their posture. Moss watched as he appraised them, sizing them up. He could see a natural mistrust under the affable demeanor.

"You plan on staying long?" he asked, but Petal answered before they had a chance.

"They mean to break someone out of C City," she said, having correctly assessed their plan. Daffodil's face grew grave a moment before returning to friendly.

"Then you shall want to visit with Captain Amakum, no doubt," he said, looking briefly at Ynna's robotic hand. "You are his type of people."

"Where can we find this captain?" Ynna asked, and Daffodil looked to his daughter.

"The saloon, as ever," she said, harsh judgment coating her words.

"I think my daughter wishes he would spend time in her company rather than that of drink," Daffodil said with a laugh.

"Daddy!" she exclaimed, turning a bright shade of red.

"Come now, Petal, there is no shame in human desire. It is the greatest strength Tellus has bestowed upon us," he said, holding up a pious finger. Infuriated, Princess Petal hustled into the castle, giving a slight bow to the visitors before disappearing.

"Heavy is the head," Daffodil intoned, shaking his head and sending beads of sweat to hiss on the wood at his feet.

"Will this captain take us at night? We have little time," Ynna asked.

"That, I do not know," the king said. "Is there anything else I can provide before consoling the light of my life?"

"No, you and your family have already shown us such kindness," Moss said.

"May Tellus grant you good fortune in your endeavors," the king said and turned, his flat rear jiggling as he ascended the steps. The guards did not drop their gaze from the three as they turned to head back to the saloon.

"Strange place," Gibbs said absently, and Moss checked to be sure the guards were out of earshot.

Ynna did not seem to care, saying, "Fucking dirt worshipers don't seem to like me all too much."

"At least we were warned," Moss said.

"I guess that's something, anyway," Ynna said, displeased with the entire place. A young man made his way up the street, lighting torches as the light of the day faded.

"The heat is brutal," Gibbs said.

"Gotta love dipshits who loathe the very technology their lives depend on," Ynna said sarcastically. "Fucking idiotic if you ask me."

Moss watched as a mother hustled her young son into a

home and away from them. It wasn't fear he saw on the woman's face, but hatred.

"I won't be sad to leave here," Gibbs agreed. "Petal was lovely, eh?"

Ynna snorted. "A real charmer."

"What did Powers give us to trade?" Moss asked, and Ynna patted the bag slung over her shoulder.

"Car pieces, repair equipment, and some small arms. Stuff he said they would like," she said.

"Gave it to us while you were on the phone," Gibbs said, "Issy still distant?"

Moss dropped his head, supposing enough time had passed to now speak of it. "Seems that way. It's all weird now," he told them quietly.

"She'll come around," Ynna offered, putting a hand on Moss's shoulder and giving a little squeeze.

"I'm not sure she should," Moss said pitifully as they walked up onto the porch of Drudge Head Saloon.

CHAPTER 10

The entire saloon was constructed of wood with a bar off to the left, a stage at the rear and tables with chairs filling the space between. The heads and arms of ThutoCo drudges hung from plaques on the wall with names and dates scrawled beneath. Hard looking men and women sat at the tables, watching a woman dance on stage. She was naked except two large feather fans she used to conceal herself as she moved. She played at shocked embarrassment as, one by one, the plumage fell away.

By the time they reached the bar, she had but a few feathers left to hide her body as she continued to dance with false modesty. The audience whooped and hollered as they approached the glistening, shirtless bartender. He was too fixated on the show to pay them any mind. Moss cleared his throat. The man's head turned before his eyes caught up, meeting Moss's gaze. A broad grin crossed his dry lips, exposing a few yellowed teeth. Staring at those teeth in a room constructed of wood, it struck Moss how truly different this place was from anything he had seen before. He had known it, experienced the differences, but something about the rotted-out teeth landed on him.

In the Burbs, teeth were perfect. Skin was perfect. Hair was anything anyone could want. The world was sterile and clean, lighted in oppressive fluorescent. Even out in the city, people cared more for how they appeared than about anything else, endlessly sending pictures and updates to uninterested friends. The city itself was concrete and glass. Nothing was natural—the human body genetically manipulated before birth and augmented after.

This town was different in every way—a bubble amidst the trees.

Moss glanced at the robot mounted on the wall behind the bar and realized this was no sanctuary. The lives here were about technology as much as in the city, only from a different point of view—loathing rather than the full embrace. Moss's momentary trance was broken.

"What can I get you city folk?" the bartender asked, his eyes darting between them and the stage.

"What's your local specialty?" Gibbs asked.

"Everything we got is local," the man said graciously. Moss had expected him to be cold and hard based on the clientele and furnishings, but he seemed genuinely happy to be serving them.

"Whatever you think is best," Gibbs said with a smile.

"What can you offer?" the bartender asked and Ynna didn't miss a beat before placing the bag on the bar and unzipping it.

"I'll never get used to a moneyless system," Gibbs said as the man rifled through the bag. He continued when no one spoke. "I mean, back at home, everything we did just came out of our paycheck which itself was determined by output. Spent my savings on digital adornments and games I'll never see again. Wild, right?"

"Ah," the bartender said, pulling a classic pistol from the

bag. "This will fix you for drinks," he said, "and dinner when it comes."

"Great," Ynna said as he put three wood cups on the bar. "Also, can you point us to Captain Am—Am—A-something? Fucking heat's getting to me."

"Right there," he said, pointing to a dark man nursing a drink and paying no attention to the woman and her two remaining feathers. The crowd cheered, and Gibbs stared as the woman was left with just her hands to cover her as she hustled from the stage before turning to give a sweeping bow.

"Like that, do you?" Ynna mocked, shoving a drink against his chest.

"What's not to like?" Gibbs protested, grabbing the cup and taking a sip. "Oh, my," he said in a scratchy voice.

"Come on, perv, we've got a job to do," Ynna said, and they walked over to the captain. A brown leather hat sat on the table next to a flickering candle, and he was dressed in all khaki. A button-up shirt rolled to the elbows and tucked into pants covered in pockets. He was muscular. Not with the vanity figure of fit men from the city, but the practical muscles which came from hard work.

"Looking for a ride?" He cocked an eyebrow as he looked up at them with red, tired eyes.

"We are," Ynna said.

"Then join me," he told them in a low voice, pushing a chair away from the table with a booted foot. They all sat. "You're on the run?"

"Something like that," Moss said.

"Wouldn't be here if you weren't," he said.

"That's true," Moss agreed. "We are looking for someone to take us to Carcer City."

"That right?" the captain said, slowly raising his cup to his lips and taking a slow sip. "Come to the right person, though perhaps at the wrong time. Anders, by the way," he added by way of introduction.

Moss introduced them before asking, "Why a bad time?"

"I'm pretty well drunk," he stated, "but I won't be forever."

"We can go in the morning," Ynna offered.

"But you wish you could go now?" he asked knowingly.

"We do, but we can wait," Moss offered, not wanting to anger their potential ride.

"If you're going to C City, I'll bet you're trying to get there first," Anders said.

"We are," Moss admitted. The man nodded.

"The princess called you captain," Gibbs put in. "You fly?"

"Not anymore," Anders said and finally raised his head to look at them. He was chiseled and handsome, the type of man Gibbs loved to complain about enviously back in the Burb. "I used to work colonial trade routes back in the day."

Ynna said, "A pirate."

"Not that there's anything wrong with that," Gibbs tried to save the moment, but Anders was grinning devilishly at Ynna.

"Yes, some would say pirate," he told them.

"Wow!" Gibbs said, unable to contain his excitement.

"Not as glamorous as you imagine," he said to Gibbs. "Got shot out of the sky in zero-g. Kind of thing makes you long for good old terrafirma."

"I'll bet," Ynna said, eyes wide as he spoke.

"C City is quite a ways away. You can pay?" he asked, and Ynna placed the bag on the table. The man smirked.

"Nothing you got in there could get you where you're going, got money?" he asked.

"A couple of million," Gibbs told him.

"So, not really." Anders snorted. "Seem able-bodied."

"We are in a hurry," Moss pressed.

"Your hurry doesn't pay my bills," Anders said, stone-faced.

"We are good in a scrap," Ynna said.

"Then I'll take that bag, a couple a million and a little help along the way," he said, and the crowd in the room complained loudly as a young boy stepped to the stage with a violin.

"Bring the girl back!" one shouted, but the kid was unfazed, lifting the instrument to his cheek. He slid the bow slowly down once, before playing at a fever pitch, creating a sound Moss had never heard before in his life. The room fell silent, all eyes glued to the boy as his fingers flashed around the strings. He began dancing about the stage, the rapid music filling the space.

"It's a hell of a thing," Anders said.

"It is," Moss mouthed, watching the kid play. The instrument twanged and stopped as the door to the saloon was kicked open by a hulking man followed by several lackeys.

"Anders!" he shouted, and every person in the room turned to look. He was tall, broad, dirty, and angry.

"Don't pull guns in here," Anders told them before standing and turning to face the man.

"You got me," he said, raising his hands. Ynna was up instantly, leaving the bag on the table. Moss and Gibbs followed her lead.

"You knew I was running that raid and you snaked it out from under me!" the red-faced man accused, the others moving in to form a semicircle at his sides.

"I remember it differently," Anders said with smiling defiance. The man moved closer, his friends closing in. Ynna made a quick series of hand motions they used during operations, indicating that she would take the three on the right and Moss and Gibbs would take the others if it came to it. They nodded nearly imperceptibly. "Why don't I buy you fellas a drink, and we can talk about it," Anders offered.

"Why don't I pull your fucking head off and ask it for a

drink?" the man threatened, moving closer. "You still have any of the loot?"

"What makes you think it was me?" Anders asked, all false innocence.

"Don't think me a fool. I know your work when I see it. Now, is there anything left? Maybe I'll go check your garage?" he said. Moss watched as Anders shifted his feet slightly. The move was unmistakable. Moss shifted as well, ready for what he knew came next.

"You have no proof and no business checking my garage," Anders said, his tone serious and deadly.

"Fine," the man said, turning away for a moment before wheeling around, his fist moving quickly toward Anders. The captain dodged left quickly, leaving the man to punch air. Anders landed a blow with his left hand, but the man could take a hit.

Ynna's foot crunched against the face of one of the lackeys, sending him reeling back and the room erupted in violence. Gibbs leaped forward, spearing one of the men to the ground as Moss punched another in the nose with a crack. The man stepped back but recovered quickly as the woman next to him swung at Moss. He moved but not quite quickly enough, taking a blow to the neck. A fist hit her in the face from Ynna who had already dispatched her three. Moss lifted a robotic leg, and it folded inward at the shin, the mock skin bunching up before he released it at the recovering man's chest. It sprang out like a shot and sent the man crashing into a table.

Anders turned to the three as the thugs tried to right themselves, "Follow me."

They did, hurrying from the bar to one of the many garages which abutted the dome wall.

"Friends of yours?" Ynna chided.

"Something like that," Anders told them, watching over his shoulder. "Lots of misunderstandings outside the cities."

"Lots of misunderstandings inside the cities, too," Moss said, "just ask the Legion."

Anders huffed derisively as he punched some numbers into a keypad, "Bikers think they're so tough. Like to see how long they last out here."

The door hissed open as the man from the saloon staggered out.

"Anders!" he shouted, "I'll find you! Be sure of that. No safe harbors left. I'll find you!"

Anders gave a hand gesture which Moss did not recognize but could understand the meaning of. They hustled into the garage and Anders had the door closing before Gibbs was even entirely through.

"Will they chase us?" Moss asked, rubbing his neck.

"No. Unwritten agreement that we won't do violence outside the domes," Anders informed them.

"Why's that?" Gibbs asked, shaking the hand he had used to pummel.

"No one deserves to get sick. You kill another person outside, and they'll hang you at the first dome you reach," he told them, switching on the lights and illuminating his van. While it was the same basic model which Martha had used, this one had been customized with care and looked more like a spaceship than a car. The thrusters had all been expanded and modified to allow for higher speeds. A layer of modifoam was set between the cab and the base for a smoother ride. Twin rows of solar panels were mounted on the top on necks which would turn to face the sun at all times. Machine guns flanked the strip of head-light which cut across the front beneath the windshield. Long fins protruded from the side and one on the top alongside an interference dish. The single word "Bess" was painted in blue on the black exterior.

"Wow," Moss thought aloud.

"She's a beaut," Anders affirmed, seeming now much less drunk than when they had met him.

"She is," Ynna exclaimed, running her fingers along the vehicle.

"I suppose you'll be getting what you wanted," Anders said, "by way of a thank you for your help in there."

Looking him up and down, Ynna said, "Doubt you needed our help."

Anders smirked, "Wouldn't want to show off so soon."

"So, you'll take us to Carcer City tonight?" Gibbs interrupted the moment.

"I will," Anders affirmed. "Though it won't take just one night's ride. I mentioned it's far."

"Does our help pay off our ride?" Moss asked hopefully.

"Not a chance," Anders chuckled, "but it helps."

"We'll leave now?" Gibbs asked.

"Unless you want to go back into town?" Anders offered with a wry smile.

"Not even at all," Gibbs said as Anders slid open the side door. The van was spacious with two long seats along the sides. A wall separated driver from passengers with a window between two screens. The space was clearly set up to transport people in style.

"There are tanks in the back, but you shouldn't need them," Anders told them as they climbed in, settling into the plush seats.

"What kind of work might we do along the way?" Moss asked.

"Wouldn't you rather be surprised?" Anders asked with a slight wink.

Moss was not in the mood for games and was worried what kind of action they might be seeing. "No."

"Well, then let's say I don't want to spoil the surprise," Anders said, sliding into the front seat and turning on the computers.

"What's with the name?" Gibbs asked, leaning forward to stick his head through the divider window as the van was foamed.

"Bess?" Anders asked.

"Yeah," Gibbs said, "your mom or something?"

"Grandma. Good guess," he responded.

"No longer with us?" Gibbs asked respectfully.

"Nah, died a long time ago on Colony 11-76. Named all my ships for her," he told them.

"You're an off-worlder?" Gibbs asked excitedly. The garage door opened, and they pulled out into the dark world.

"Yes," Anders told them.

"Were you involved in the revolts?" Gibbs asked, and while both Moss and Ynna played it cool, they were listening intently.

"How old do you think I am?" Anders chuckled. "That was well before my time. The corporate breakaway happened when my parents were children."

"Oh," Gibbs said, disappointed. "I've just never met an off-worlder."

"Well, before you get dreams of spacemen and the free lives in the stars, let me tell you, it's exactly the same out there as down here," he said.

"But the colonists rebelled against the companies," Gibbs said, quoting from his company history class. Anders laughed.

He snorted. "That what they teach you? Guessing they left out the part where they rebelled simply to form their own corporate entities so a whole new slew of people could get rich."

Gibbs looked embarrassed. "No."

"Traded the yoke of one master for another, just rebranded," Anders said, and while it was not at all surprising, it was disappointing.

While teaching of the revolt, ThutoCo had presented the whole situation as an ugly affair where the colonists didn't realize how good they had it. After escaping the Burbs, he thought of the revolt as being enacted by noble freedom fighters trying to rid themselves of their oppressors.

"You ever want to return?" Ynna asked.

"Not any time soon," Anders said in a tone which suggested the conversation had come to a close. When Gibbs did not lean back, he added, "Why don't you all lay down for a bit. I'll get us a good distance before stopping. We'll have a full day tomorrow."

"I'll take the floor," Moss offered, noting that it was padded as well. He took one last look out the window, appreciating how truly dark it was. In the Burbs and city, even the dark wasn't dark —small, flickering LED lights, and the blue glow of screens seeped into everything. Out here, out in the wilderness, it was all black.

"No argument here," Ynna said and sprawled out on one of the seats. Gibbs did the same, and it was not long before they were all sleeping in a car once more.

CHAPTER 11

Sun filtered into the van as dark shades lifted slowly.

"I think I've slept too much," Ynna moaned groggily.

"Some pep?" Anders asked from the front, extending a hand with a bottle.

"What is it?" Gibbs asked, raising himself slowly and grabbing the bottle, sloshing the unnaturally green liquid.

Anders grinned with a sweeping gesture toward the sky. "A secret from the stars."

"Fine, keep your secrets," Gibbs said in a light voice and uncorked the bottle.

"What's the day looking like?" Moss asked suggestively, still hoping he would simply take them directly to Carcer City.

"Going to run a quick job, stop by a town and be on our way," Anders stated.

Moss had known it was coming but had hoped they might have gotten out of it. "What kind of a quick job?"

"Standard smash and grab, no big thing for people like you, I think," he said implicitly.

Ynna raised an eyebrow. "People like us?"

"Yes," Anders said bluntly, "capable people."

"We are that," Ynna affirmed with a smirk.

"I know it. What'd you take down, four?" he asked her, and it was the closest to blushing Moss had ever seen from her.

"We are—" Ynna began.

"Good in a scrap," Anders finished.

"So, you weren't that drunk." She beamed, and Anders shot a devilish grin.

"I'm never that drunk. Just needed to size you up before granting passage. This isn't some luxury liner," he explained.

"Right." Ynna snorted, patting the seat beside her. "I'm sure it's a lot of rough and tumble folks who usually ride back here."

"Sure, I provide a nice ride to some nice people, but I didn't know you all from a hole in the ground and—" it was Ynna's turn to cut him off.

"We were trying to cop a ride on the cheap," she said, and he simply smiled and shot a wink. He pressed a button and the monitors in the back came to life, showing two newscasters sitting before an image of BA City.

"That's right, Bernard," one anchor said. "The Miners pulled out a one-to-nil win over the Docksmen, securing their place in the cup semi-finals. Here's a shot of the celebration on Market Street when time ran down." They cut to a scene of celebration in the streets, people cheering and screaming as they watched the giant holoscreen. Speeding through fields far from the city, hoping to break their friends out of prison before they met grue-some ends, Moss couldn't believe the ecstasy he watched. A city, whose friends and loved ones had been saved by them, all bliss-fully unaware of what was happening.

He remembered being ten years old before his parents had been taken. His mom had been rushed to surgery for a heart condition. They had been ushered from the room, his father taking his hand and walking him to a nearby café in the Burb. Moss had watched in amazement as people went about their days. He couldn't believe that normal life persisted during something so devastating to him.

The crowd erupted again as they showed footage of the point being scored.

"So, what will you need from us?" Moss asked.

"A little help," Anders said.

"Is there a reason you're being so fucking coy?" Ynna asked, and Moss smiled. Sometimes he really appreciated how forthright she was.

"Because there is no reason to jaw about it when we can just do the thing," Anders argued.

"Burn would have loved this one," Gibbs said with an exaggerated eye roll.

Ynna snorted. "No kidding."

"Friend of yours?" Anders asked.

"Yeah," Moss said, "no-nonsense type."

"Dead?" he asked.

Moss looked at his feet, remembering his friend and mentor covered in blood in the basement of ThutoCo headquarters. "Yeah."

"Sorry. Sounds like my kinda guy," Anders said respectfully. "If you guys want to grab packs and get geared, we can get this going."

They all moved to a locker at the rear of the cab and began pulling the oxygen tanks on.

"Do we need to worry about our clothes?" Gibbs asked.

"Doesn't seem to work that way," Anders informed them. "We rinse our cars to be safe, but it's more just a precaution."

Ynna scowled. "Someone needs to get some actual fucking answers about all this."

"If ThutoCo was weaponizing it, pretty sure they know everything," Moss pointed out, and Ynna seemed to ponder his words.

"You two aren't seriously considering breaking back in when we have Carcer to deal with?" Gibbs asked.

"No shit?" Anders raised an eyebrow, understanding what Gibbs's words implied.

Ynna shot Gibbs a withering look before saying, "Yeah."

Anders smiled slightly. "This world owes you a debt."

"A debt you have no interest in paying I presume," Moss said as he clipped the tank across his chest.

"Correct you are," Anders chuckled, "but I appreciate what you folks have done."

"What's the plan?" Gibbs asked. He sounded nervous and was pulling at the hair at the back of his neck.

"We are going to break in and steal some shit," Anders told them. Moss looked at the clock and smiled, seeing the time.

"From ThutoCo," Gibbs said.

"Yes," Anders said. "Figured you'd like that bit."

Moss had a distant look, the wheels in his mind turning. "Smart," he observed, turning his eyes to Anders.

"What is?" Anders asked, though his smirk suggested that he understood.

"We're going in at shift change," Moss said plainly.

Anders gave a clever look and winked. "Right."

"What are you two on about?" Ynna asked, sounding impatient as she tapped her fingers on her knees.

"There is a window between night and morning shifts when the drudges go offline to run internal diagnostics so they can inform their new controllers of any damage. If they are the dedicated drudges which are rewarded to high-level employees, they go offline completely for the day," Moss told her. "On the ground level, we always complained about this gap and the fact that the scubas could take advantage of it. Management never seemed to care, but it was an obvious failing."

"And someone was smart enough to take advantage," Ynna said.

"As he said, it was fairly obvious," Anders said modestly. "Call us scubas because of the tanks?"

"Yes," Moss affirmed.

"Not a lot of thought went into that one, eh?" Anders mocked.

"I didn't come up with it!" Moss defended.

Anders raised his hands defensively and looked over to a chuckling Gibbs. "I hit a nerve?"

"Sure did," Ynna affirmed with a smile.

"Ready to roll?" Anders asked, mercifully dropping the subject, and they all nodded. He drove them down the crest of a hill to an automated chain-link fence, pulling out a tablet and making short work of the controls. The gate rattled open quickly, and the camera lights turned from red to green.

"Just that easy?" Ynna asked.

"Never been hard to get passwords for a price. A whole lot easier now that the employees know their bosses wanted to kill them," Anders said with a smile, pulling into the ThutoCo repair yard. The cameras did not turn to follow the vehicle, and no drones left their nests. The drudges sat silently as they pulled up to a large, open hanger door. He backed up and indicated for everyone to put on their respirators.

After they did, he hopped out and came around, opening the door and pointing at some boxes on pallets. Gibbs and Ynna moved quickly as Moss took a moment to look around. The whole place was so familiar. He had spent so many days working in places like this. He looked to the bank of monitors where he would have work orders uploaded to MOSS II, seeing it was in standby.

"I thought you hacked the security?" Moss asked, his voice muffled and tinny.

"I did. Turned it off," Anders said, and Moss gripped his Kingfisher.

"We have to get out of here!" Moss shouted, but the sound of approaching drones was already beginning to buzz.

"Guess management finally listened," Anders said as he threw the boxes into the back of the van. "Stand and fight or try and get out?"

"Take the first wave from here then get the fuck out," Moss ordered, and everyone readied their weapons at his command. The drudges came to life, all of them fitted with hidden weaponry, tasers appearing from wrists and shoulders. Anders continued to load boxes as Moss blasted the nearest drudge, shattering plastic and glass with the powerful new weapon.

Gibbs raised his long rifle, firing multiple shots into the air and sending three drones careening to the ground with tails of smoke. Ynna dodged and weaved as several drudges took aim, firing blue bolts at her which hissed and popped as they missed their target. Her rifle popped as more robots crashed to the ground.

"You plan on helping?" she shouted at Anders as he loaded the final box and slid the door closed. He wheeled around and shot a drudge in the head with a long-barreled silver pistol. He raised the weapon with calm determination and shot two drones from the sky.

"Patience is a virtue, my dear," he said as he twisted at the waist to avoid a shot. More drones moved in, and Gibbs fired wildly, taking down one before another shot Ynna in the neck. She began convulsing instantly, and Moss rushed to her side, firing an unnecessary number of shots into a nearby drudge.

The machine burst into electric fire, sending plumes of smoke into the air as it fell. Moss checked to be sure her respirator was still in place and began to move her. Gibbs and Anders covered Moss as he heaved Ynna toward the van.

Gibbs rushed to his side, grabbing Ynna's legs, and snorting. "Lucky she's light."

"Cover us," Moss screamed to Anders, though he already was, and they lifted her limp body into the van. Anders shot down the final drudge and had to reload. A drone fired a blue blast which struck Moss in the chest. His shirt burned but the bodysuit autocorrected, distributing the charge harmlessly.

"Thank you, Powers," Moss huffed, the impact of the shot having knocked his breath. Anders shot down the last two drones.

"Let's go," he said as he jumped into the van. "Lucky they didn't think to shoot the car."

"They may now," Moss observed as the vehicle pulled from the yard.

"Got any stims?" Gibbs asked as he pulled the mouthpiece away from Ynna's face.

"Sorry," Anders said, "you can splash her, but I'd just let her sleep it off."

"Let's get this tank off," Gibbs said as he worried the clips.

"Take a deep breath," Moss advised. "She'll be fine."

"Sure," he answered, worry betraying him, "it's just—"

"I know," Moss finished.

"Something going on between you two?" Anders asked, watching the screen for any sign of further drones.

Gibbs flushed and admitted, "No."

"Good," Anders said, and Gibbs grimaced.

"I mean, there could be," Gibbs added quietly.

"Not really your call, though, is it?" Anders said.

"No," Gibbs nearly whispered, and now it was Moss's turn to grimace. He thought it was distraction enough the way Gibbs and Ynna carried on and didn't need another interference.

"Any sign of activity?" he asked, trying to change the subject.

It worked. "Not yet," Anders said, tapping the radar. "We're cloaked now, but we give off heat signatures."

"Got a couple of tricks up your sleeve?" Moss asked, and he saw Anders grin.

"I'm a pilot, right?" he said suggestively.

"Thought you were a captain?" Gibbs said derisively, and Anders said nothing.

"So, where are the boxes going?" Moss asked, hooking a thumb in their direction. He was more exhausted from dealing with the nonsense between them than being in a gunfight.

"Town not far from here," he told them. "And before you ask, we'll be on our way to C City after."

"Good," Moss said and added, "thank you."

"I'd have been up a creek without your help back there, so no thanks are needed. This is an exchange," Anders said cooly. Moss couldn't figure the man. He acted casual around them and friendly at times, but there was something in the man—quiet sadness behind the eyes which would seep out in the silent moments.

"Anders," Moss began, setting a tone. "How long have you been on earth?"

"Why do you ask?" Anders sounded more genuinely curious than evasive.

Moss thought about it a moment. "We've been in two fights together in less than a day, figured I should get to know you."

"Fair enough. I've been here about two years. Spent a little time in SeaWa fixing ships, running odd jobs, but the city life wasn't for me. We have cities back home, and they're all the same—too many people, not enough space. I'm already accustomed to bottled oxygen, so this part of the planet makes sense for me. I like open spaces, even when they're viewed from confined ones," he said, clearly thinking as he spoke.

"That," Moss said, "I can understand."

"Live in the city your whole life?" Anders asked, and even Gibbs smiled. Since leaving, everyone had known they were from the Burbs instantly, and it was refreshing to be asked if they were from the city.

"No," Moss admitted, "born and raised in a ThutoCo Burb. They took my father when they realized he was working from the inside to destroy their plans. I was a kid, and they wiped my memory of the whole affair. The company raised me, and I would have died there if it hadn't been for her and her friends."

He pointed to Ynna.

"Now you're, what, a freedom fighter trying to save the world from tyrannical corporations?" he asked, sounding more condescending than he likely meant to. Moss laughed.

"Something like that," he said as they crested a small rise, looking down into a valley with a grass-covered hill in the center. As they neared, large circular windows set into the hill became visible. A tower pointed out of the top with dishes on all sides.

"Wow," Gibbs said, "you know what it looks like?"

"Yeah," Moss agreed, knowing what his friend meant without having to say it.

Anders furrowed his brow, looking back and forth between the two. "What?"

"Nothing," Moss smiled, "an old movie."
"Ah, we don't get those off-world. When NeoVerge Industries broke away, they destroyed any reminders of earth. Created all new content to keep us from longing for a home we never knew," Anders said.

"That's miserable," Gibbs observed, sounding genuinely sad for them.

"It works," Anders pointed out, "give people food, a bed, and a screen, and you've got a slave for life."

Moss knew the truth in his words. If this life had not come

crashing through his door, he would have spent his entire life as a worker bee watching Burbz Haz Skillz until he died.

They pulled toward a bank of round doors and pulled through one. There were no guards, only cameras with mounted gun turrets. The camera shifted as the vehicle pulled in. The door rolled closed behind them, and the van was washed as they moved to a well-lighted garage.

"I'll wait with her," Gibbs offered, and Anders nodded.

He turned to Moss. "You'll help me offload?"

"Certainly," Moss said, happy to separate the two from one another.

They hopped out, and Anders pointed to an automated pallet in the corner of the enclosed cement space. They heaved the boxes onto the pallet, and Anders turned on the control. It took a while, and Moss watched as Anders pulled a small bag from the front seat which he quickly hid away in his jacket.

"Ready?" Anders asked as he turned a key in the pallet operator, the square hovering off the ground.

"I'm honestly excited to see what it looks like inside," Moss told him, and he meant it.

"You should be," Anders smirked.

CHAPTER 12

Walking through the bowels of this dome was a completely different experience than the last. Winding corridors of dripping pipes stretched on and on for what seemed to be interminable. It was slow going, the pallet having a low top speed to prevent workplace injuries. They eventually reached a glass elevator, and Anders turned with a broad smile, "I think you're going to like this."

Moss didn't know what to make of the comment and pushed the button to go up a floor. Light filled the elevator as they rose into another world. Moss gasped. They lifted into a dome within the dome, surrounded by water filled with brightly colored fish. The underwater creatures flitted and darted about as the elevator slid into place. Moss pressed his hands to the glass, staring at the animals.

"How?" he exclaimed, childlike enthusiasm coating the word.

"Labor of love," Anders remarked.

"Clones?" Moss asked, expecting an answer.

"Nope," Anders said, pleased with Moss's happiness. "Call

themselves The Conservation, work to keep the critters alive. Apparently, this was some kind of research facility before the disease."

Moss looked around, hardly able to speak. "Remarkable."

"It is," Anders agreed, and the doors slid open, pulling Moss's attention to a man and a little girl in matching green pants and khaki shirts.

"Anders!" the girl shouted and ran into his awaiting arms.

"Captain," the man acknowledged and turned to Moss. "I'm Administrator Chester, and this is my daughter, Amy."

"Good to meet you both," Moss said, shaking the man's hand. "I'm Moss."

"Moss," Chester repeated, "great name. It might interest you to know that we have a small Japanese moss garden with over two hundred species from the Yatsugatake mountain range with some truly beautiful Polystichum Juniperinum growing there. I think you would love it."

"I think I would," Moss agreed, having no idea what the words meant or where the mountain range was. "What else do you have here?"

"Oh, my," Chester said, stoking his cleanly shaved chin. "Quite a lot. The exact numbers change constantly but over two hundred species of animals, not counting the fish and over one thousand types of flora and fauna. Our mission is to protect these wild things for a day when we let this planet return to a natural state."

Moss's eyes grew wide at the thought. "Wonderful."

He watched as Anders slipped the bag from his jacket into the young girl's hands and realized it was a small fish in the bag. Anders shot her a wink and tussled her hair before she skipped off excitedly.

"What'd you bring her this time?" Chester asked with a kindly smile.

"Just a little something I picked up," Anders said in affected coyness.

"You're incorrigible." Chester laughed. "This it?" he asked, pointing to the boxes.

"Yes, but I won't be able to get you much more for a while, I think. ThutoCo got wise," Anders said.

"Bound to happen," Chester said sullenly. "This should last us a while though, get it into the hands of the engineers and we'll be back up and running."

"Good to hear," Anders said.

"And as for payment?" Burr asked.

"Same as always," Anders replied, shifting uncomfortably.

Chester seemed to pick up on the energy and looked at Moss, "Anything I can get you? Would you like to take a look around?"

"Yes!" Moss answered without thinking, turning to Anders and covering, "Ynna's probably still out, so we have some time."

"Sure." Anders chuckled. "And I could eat. Asshole came at me before the food came."

Moss became aware of his own hunger, "We should bring some back for them, too."

"We will," Anders said. "Chester, you willing to take him around and feed him and I'll take this down to engineering?"

"Sure thing," Chester said.

"Catch you in a bit," Anders said to Moss.

"Follow me," Chester said, leading Moss down the corridor which led from the elevator. He waved a keycard, and a door hissed open. Moss's heart nearly jumped from his chest. He turned into a room of metal pathways hung over an open pool from the roof of the dome with its massive circular windows fitted with light distributors that illuminated the room in bright, natural light. Waves lapped against the walls and fish moved between the corals deep below. Glass tanks were set on open platforms with small habitats within. Colorful birds squawked as they flew overhead to land on large cement perches cut to resemble tree limbs.

Two glass balls the size of buildings sat on either side of the room, filled with trees and animals which moved between the leaves.

Moss, mouth agape said, "It's like a Burb for animals."

Chester laughed, "I've never thought of it in those particular terms. We keep them alive and as genetically diverse as we can for a potential release someday. Many things must change in the interim, though."

"Yes," Moss agreed, wishing he could simply snap his fingers and change the world. Guilt struck him then. For as much as he wanted to stay, gawking and speaking to all the people taking notes on tablets, he knew his friends were in dire need. This whole journey had taken longer than he had hoped, and he needed to help his crew. "Perhaps we should eat and be on our way," he said miserably.

"Sure," Chester said as a shark moved slowly under the platform at their feet. He guided Moss to a large cafeteria where people sat in their uniformed attire, eating and chatting. They both got plates of salad and sat at a long table. "Seen any wildlife on your trip?" Chester asked, looking in Moss's eyes.

He was older than Moss by about ten years, he guessed, and of a slender build, with curious green eyes. His skin appeared to have never seen the sunlight except for that which filtered through the windows. Moss told him of the bears and the feeling of wonderment which struck him at seeing them.

Chester nodded along and put some information into a tablet after asking where Moss thought the animals had been located.

After a brief moment of silence, Moss sheepishly asked, "Are there elephant seals here?"

"No," Chester said with a sullen smile. "Animals of that size require more space than we can provide."

"Oh," Moss's face dropped.

"You seem very interested in the natural world," Chester observed.

"I'm coming to realize how true that is," Moss agreed.

"We always need more hands," Chester offered, and Moss smiled.

"Maybe one day," he said, and he meant it, "but I have a lot of work to do."

Chester looked at him with interest. "I imagine you do."

A moment of silence passed between them before Moss asked what he had been wanting to for a while. "Have you known Anders long?"

Chester shifted slightly, clearly unsure how much to divulge.

"A while, yes," Chester said before deflecting, "he's very good with my daughter."

"I saw that." Moss nodded. "You think he has children?"

"I think you could ask him," Chester said before thinking better of his answer. "Look, Moss, I don't know you, but you seem a good sort, and I can tell you the captain is, too. He is kind and honorable, and I know it would pain him for me to tell you, but he gathers supplies for us for free. Sure, he'll take a room or a meal but never asks for more than that."

"I got that sense," Moss told him.

"And I think if he had children, they are gone now," Chester added, poking at his salad without looking up.

"You think he would help strangers simply because it was the right thing to do?" Moss asked, getting to the heart of it.

"I do," Chester said and began eating his salad.

THEY CHATTED IDLY A WHILE LONGER, speaking of plants and

animals. Chester got Moss some food in containers he could take back before beginning to walk back toward the elevator.

"You think I could see that moss room?" Moss asked quietly.

"Of course," Chester affirmed easily, and they turned down a long corridor to another glass room. "Would you like a minute?"

"Yes, thank you," Moss said, and Chester waved him in. The smell of wet earth filled his nose, and a few birds pecked about as Moss sat on a small bench in one corner. Except for a slight gravel path, the room was fully green. All the rocks and logs were covered with fine green fur. He thought about the AI construct of his father which he lost in the explosions at ThutoCo HQ.

"I hope this is what you wanted," he said aloud. "I hope you are proud of what I've done, of what I'm doing. We brought down ThutoCo, but they are fighting back, and there is so much more that needs to be done. I've tried my best to be good and honorable, but I know I've failed. People have died, others taken. I'm not sure how to earn their sacrifices, but I'm trying. I found your mother. I'm trying to help her. I hope that counts for something."

His voice echoed off the glass, staying with him after he spoke. He knew his father was dead. Knew he was alone, but it helped him to say the words out loud. He gritted his teeth and steeled himself for the road ahead. He understood he was up against impossible odds—breaking into a prison to free several people who Carcer valued.

It would be tough, and he might not survive, but he owed it to them to try. As he stood, he saw a small bumpy green frog spotted with brown sitting on his shoe. He looked down and smiled, but as he went to pick it up, it hopped toward a small burbling pond.

"I'll do what I can to give you your world back," he said, turning away from the room.

. . .

ANDERS WAS STANDING with Chester when Moss left the room.

"Ready to go?" Anders asked, food slung under one arm.

"Not really, but yes," Moss answered truthfully.

"As I said, you are always welcome," Chester said kindly, extending a hand.

Moss looked around once more. "I truly hope to return."

"I think that you will," he said and turned to Anders, "a pleasure as always. Thanks for Amy's gift. I'm sure you've made her day."

"Certainly hope so," Anders said, genuine kindness in his words.

"Good luck, gentlemen," and he left them. Moss looked at Anders.

"I imagine she's awake by now," Anders said.

"Let's get going then." Moss was sad to leave but ready to help his friends. They walked back to the elevator in silence. As they descended, Moss cleared his throat a bit awkwardly.

Anders raised an eyebrow. "Yes?"

"I have a question, and you are under no obligation. I mean, I know you know that, but I just mean, well, I was hoping," he stuttered, his words failing him when he needed them most.

Anders held up a calming hand. "You want my help when we get to C City?"

Moss let out a deep sigh of relief. "Yes."

"And you want it for free?" he asked.

"We have nothing to offer you now, but after," he began, but Anders shook his head.

"Listen, I know you're up against it, and I know you are trying to do good. I'll help you. But not for money or rewards. I'll help you because I can," he said.

Something seemed to have changed in the man. Some altruistic switch had been flipped, and Moss guessed he had the little girl to thank.

Moss looked into Anders's bright, chestnut eyes. "Thank you."

"Don't thank me yet. I could work for Carcer and be leading you to your death," he said in mock seriousness.

"Don't put that thought in my head. We were having a nice moment!" Moss exclaimed, smiling as they moved down the hall plastered with safety information. He liked Anders. He was happy that he had agreed to help, for all he had done and for bringing him here, but more than that, Moss just liked how he was—tough but easy to talk to.

Anders chuckled. "Just keeping you on your toes."

"I'm always on my toes," Moss remarked, and he felt that those words were truer than just about anything. Even in the moments of calm between missions or on pointless days just lounging around, Moss was never truly able to relax. He realized he probably hadn't since leaving the burbs.

"Bet you are," Anders said, still chuckling to himself.

"While I'm asking favors," Moss added.

"Gotta push your luck?" Anders quipped.

Moss shrugged. "May as well."

"You want me to lay off Ynna?" he asked knowingly.

"Yes," Moss said, "it's just—"

"That your friend is smitten. Yeah, I see it. She sees it, too, not for nothing. I could lay off, but if she wants a piece, I'm not one to refuse a lady," Anders put bluntly.

Moss huffed. "Fair enough."

"Trust me, nothing will make up a person's mind faster than you trying to make it up for them," Anders advised. "Life will play itself out."

"Right," Moss said, no longer thinking about Gibbs and Ynna.

"Hit on something there, did I?" Anders asked as they neared the garage.

Moss looked up at him, stopping in front of the door. "That obvious?"

"That obvious," Anders replied. They entered the garage as Ynna stretched and Gibbs fiddled with his rifle. Gibbs's eyes widened as he saw the food in Moss's arms. He hustled over.

"Salad," he whined.

"You could use a fucking salad," Ynna retorted. "Gimme that."

"Anders has agreed to lend a hand," Moss announced.

"Swell," Ynna said through a mouth full of roughage, "he's good in a scrap, too."

"I may be able to be of some service," Anders offered, standing up tall and resting a fist on a hip.

Ynna rolled her eyes. "Moss fill you in on the plan?"

Anders smirked. "Do you have a plan?"

"Need to see the place first," Moss told them. "We have some Carcer gear though, so hopefully that will help."

"Fake prisoner transfer?" Gibbs suggested.

"Let's wait and see," Moss told him.

Ynna nodded toward the ceiling. "How was it up there?"

"Amazing," Moss said. "We should come back someday when we have time."

"Right," Ynna scoffed.

"Also, it turns out our new friend here has a heart of gold," Moss said, and Anders grumbled.

"Fucking Chester," he moaned.

Moss smirked. "Fucking Chester."

Anders snorted. "Let's get you to C City before any other secrets get out."

"I'm fine, by the way," Ynna announced.

"It's you. Of course, you are," Moss said and added with a wink, "it's why we don't ask."

"Asshole," Ynna said, and they all got in the van on their way to Carcer City.

CHAPTER 13

C arcer City was a sprawl of rust. Layers of walls and guard towers surrounded the brown city built into a low valley. Buildings filled every available space, and plumes of smoke rose in hundreds of acrid pillars. Drones and gunships circled like vultures. Lights from the towers scanned over the city and the people within.

Though it was a massive space, it looked small compared to BA City. None of the buildings were taller than a few stories, and they all looked dilapidated, made of scavenged materials which the jailers provided. In the center of the city lay a massive square building illuminated with floodlights and walled in. It was a command post, barrack, and interrogation center.

A single road led to an immense gate system with a medieval-style portcullis. Small cement pillboxes were built into the ground under the tall misters which surrounded the entire city. It looked as impregnable as Moss had feared.

"Fake prisoner transfer may actually be our best shot," Anders said, "I suppose it's a classic for a reason."

Gibbs beamed. "Told you."

"You said you have Carcer gear, what is it?" Anders asked.

They were parked on a hillside just outside of scanning range, though Anders had turned on all the vans defenses to be safe.

"We have a couple of prisoner's jumpsuits," Ynna said.

"That's it?" Anders asked.

"That's pretty good!" Ynna exclaimed.

Moss looked around in disappointment, stating the obvious. "We'll need more than that."

"Got a plan?" Anders asked.

"Yes," Moss said, turning to Gibbs, "think you can hit a moving target with a tank on?"

"Shot those drones down, didn't I?" Gibbs answered easily.

WITHIN AN HOUR, the three sat in the van with their tanks at the ready and Gibbs lay on an elevated spot watching the road. Utilizing the bodysuit given to him by Powers, his presence was cloaked both visually and on scanners. Moss was grateful the man had let them take such advanced tech with them.

Several prisoner transports had entered the city in the time they had been watching, and they had little doubt that another would be arriving soon. Anders had set a graymaker by the side of the road to interfere with transmissions and was watching for any activity on the radar. Moss and Ynna sat primed, ready to move at a moment's notice.

It occur to anyone that another car could come upon us leaving the city, Gibbs asked through the neural network Anders had established.

Hopefully, we'll be lucky, Moss answered.

Have we ever been? Ynna asked.

Who votes we don't think about it? Anders said, and Moss and Ynna raised their hands. *Car approaching*, and they all stopped communicating.

Moss turned to watch his friend. It was all up to Gibbs now. He surveyed through the sight—thermal images.

Four people in the transport, two in front, two in the back, he told them, and Moss watched as the weapon followed the transport, raising and lowering slightly to compensate for subtle movements. Moss was relieved that Gibbs had taken all the time to practice and believed in his friend.

Luck may be on our side, Gibbs said and took in a long breath, waiting for the vehicle to come into range.

It glided over the road, and Gibbs pressed his finger to the side of the trigger. He had one shot, one chance to hit his target. If he missed and the guards were alerted to their presence, it would all be over. An army of prison guards would swarm and take them if not kill them. He had to shake those thoughts from his mind.

The transport came within range, and Gibbs pulled the trigger, clearly aiming for where he hoped the driver would be rather than where he was. Anders had told them that Carcer used human drivers after one too many transports had been hacked.

The rifle cracked, and nothing happened for what felt like an interminable amount of time.

The transport ground to a halt.

Nice shot! Ynna told Gibbs, and their van was speeding down to the roadside.

They all hopped out quickly and surrounded the transport, guns up. Through the blood-soaked windshield, they watched as the guard tried frantically to hail the city on comms to no avail. Part of the Carcer guard armor was a built-in respirator, but she looked frantically at the small bullet hole in the windshield. Reality set in on her face, and she lifted her hands in surrender. As Anders approached the side door, her eyes narrowed briefly, and she reached for her gun. Ynna took one shot, splitting the woman's face at the bridge of her nose. Blood began to seep into the armor, and Ynna hurried to the door which was locked.

"Shit," she said as one of her fingers opened at the tip to reveal lockup picking apparatus. She fiddled quickly and got the door open. The prisoners at the back pulled at their chains, and Moss's heart broke for them as their faces were completely uncovered.

"It'll be a mercy," Anders said, seeing Moss's reaction. Gibbs came running down the hill, shimmering out of digitally rendered invisibility.

"You guys see that?" he asked excitedly before seeing the grim expressions on the faces of the three. Moss pointed to the two horrified prisoners.

"No," Gibbs said.

Ynna looked at him, her face stern. "It's too late for them anyway."

"No!" Gibbs repeated. His eyes darted around, looking for one of them to support him.

"You want to watch them suffer?" Anders asked.

"But," Gibbs began, all the color drained from his face.

"It's not your fault," Moss told him, but he was beginning to shake.

"It—it is," he said, and Moss had never seen his friend so forlorn. Tears were welling in his eyes as he realized his bullet meant certain death for two innocent people.

"We have to do this, and we don't have time for a discussion," Anders said and made his way to the back of the transport.

Ynna walked over to Gibbs.

Gibbs stared at the prisoners. "Why weren't they in masks?"

"Turn away," Ynna said softly, putting a hand on his shoulder.

"But—" He wept, and she pulled him in for an embrace.

"It's a mercy," Moss found himself repeating as he pulled his Kingfisher from its holster and followed Anders to the side door. A young woman with crimson hair flailed and thrashed.

"I'll fucking kill you!" she screamed at them. The man sitting next to her had stopped struggling and looked at them with miserable eyes. Moss stared at the two wondering what his father would think of him now?

"I'll take her," Moss said.

"Easier on the conscience?" Anders asked, and Moss simply nodded. "All right."

Moss uncoupled the woman's neck restraints and pulled her from the car.

"I'm sorry," he said as she tried to bite him, looking wild and enraged.

"Fuck you," she screamed, and he looked away as he pulled the trigger. The large man waved Anders over with a shackled hand, and Anders leaned in as he whispered something. Anders nodded, and the man went calmly to his death. Gibbs sobbed into Ynna's shoulder as Anders' pistol fired.

"I don't get it!" Gibbs shouted, his voice strained through the respirator. "If it's airborne, what good are the misters. Is it a disease, a bacteria, what? How can they do this?"

His face was wet, red, and contorted with anger and misery. Anders turned, his face severe.

"ThutoCo are liars and thieves. They and their cohorts poisoned this planet to sell goods in space. They probably have a treatment, a cure, but we will never know. We probably won't even find out how this infection works. But it doesn't matter now. What matters is helping your friends, right?"

Gibbs nodded, though his demeanor did not change.

"Ynna, it's a girl and a black guy, so it's you and me as the prisoners. These two will be the guards.

"One of the guards was a woman, too," Ynna protested.

"Yes, but Moss is... *slender*... so he can fit in that armor. So, unless someone runs the ID number, we should be alright," Anders explained. "We got a lot to do so we have to get moving —and Gibbs, I understand you blame yourself, but I just executed a man for some folks I've never met, so you have to deal with your shit later. Let's move these bodies and get back to the van before someone spots this."

His words were enough to get everyone moving. They dragged the bodies and moved the transport up to the van to keep it out of sight. One by one, they dressed in their new attire, Ynna grousing that, "We didn't even need what Powers gave us after all."

Moss looked to Anders, "I need you to break my nose."

"What?" Anders asked.

"My suit's all covered in blood. We'll just say Gibbs got blood on his from me, but we can't show up looking like this," he explained.

"I mean, I just met you, but all right," he said, shaking out his hand. Before Moss could brace himself, he felt hard metal crash against his face. Ynna laughed as Moss reeled back, pressing his hands to his face guard to try and stem the flow of blood.

"If I have to play the prisoner, I get to punch your fucking face," she said happily.

Anders laughed. "Thanks. Felt wrong to punch him."

"You both suck," Moss said. He tasted blood as it seeped out of his nose. He spit into the mask and regretted his decision. "I'll try not to make your restraints too tight."

"I could still kick your ass," Ynna chided.

"Let's do this," Gibbs said. He looked serious and threatening in the black and red plated Carcer armor. Moss realized he must look the same. He had dressed in such haste he hadn't taken the moment to appreciate the dark visage of which he appeared. He had kept the Dermidos on under the tight-fitting shirt and trousers with affixed plastimesh plates which folded into one another to keep the wearer's body mostly covered.

At his side was holstered a Turaco Brand knee-knocker. The pistol was made by the Kingfisher company's North American subsidiary for mass production. They were almost exclusively used by Carcer and were notoriously unreliable—a fact which had come in handy for Moss on more than one occasion.

The bleeding had subsided, though his face throbbed and he knew bruising would be obvious under his eyes—the only exposed portion of his body.

They shackled Ynna and Anders into the back, and Moss took the driver's seat. Stan had been teaching him how to operate a car in case of emergencies, but he didn't feel comfortable at all.

"You going to be okay?" Gibbs asked as the vehicle started moving with jerky motions.

"Are you?" Moss whispered, trying to drive smoothly.

"I don't know," Gibbs said. "I'm not sure I'm built for all this."

"I know," Moss soothed, "but things are about to get a whole lot tougher."

Gibbs nodded, and Anders announced from the back, "When we arrive, each one of you will take one of us to the transfer point."

"Right," Moss said.

"I've known people who bought their way out," Ynna told them, though Moss knew she had done time. "The guards can come and go anywhere in the city, so get a lay of the land and try to find us or the others."

"You know of any landmarks or anything in the city?" Moss asked before realizing his blunder. "Through your connections, I mean."

"There used to be a bar called the Alco-Traz. We'll make our way there tomorrow after processing," Ynna said, and Anders' face suggested he had deduced what Moss already knew about her.

"There are bars there?" Gibbs asked, seeming only just to have noticed they were speaking.

Ynna looked at him as though he was an idiot. "Sure, it's a proper city. It's just that the citizens are inmates, and everything is made from scrap and shit Carcer provides. But the people try to make lives for themselves while they wait for their family to scrounge up enough money to buy their freedom."

"What's the currency?" Gibbs asked. "A pack of smokes?"

"Money. Since Carcer sells everything used in the city to the people, the inmates use what little money they have to buy goods," Ynna told them.

"Wait," Moss said. "So, Carcer gets a bounty from whatever company or government wants a person arrested. Then they take money from the families to keep them alive and expect the inmates to pay for whatever they need to survive? Fucking profit on all sides."

Ynna snorted. "Yep, it's a pretty efficient system."

"The few companies left down here know nothing better than how to turn a profit," Anders said, fiddling with his restraints, "it's why the rebellion caught them so off guard... and what you all did. They're not used to their peons taking actions against them."

"Hopefully that's why this will work, too," Moss added.

"Shit," Gibbs said.

Moss turned nervously, before feeling the transport drift and looking back to the road. "What?"

"Will they genomatch you guys? Will they be able to tell you aren't who you say?" he worried, but Ynna chuckled.

"Nah, if they did that at all, it would have been upon arrest. We are not high priority enough to warrant it. They'll just ask you to transfer our data," she explained.

As they passed under the misters, the windshield was coated with drops of liquid and Moss panicked for a moment before the transport's internal computer compensated and dried the window. Moss decided that he hated driving.

"Good." Gibbs sighed. "Could this plan work?"

"Getting in is the easy part," Ynna said.

"This was easy?" Gibbs exclaimed.

"Easier, anyway," she corrected. "Getting out will be a lot harder."

CHAPTER 14

Moss's heart pounded as he pulled up to the gates of Carcer City. He slammed the car to a stop as a guard approached, and Moss rolled the window down. The guard inputted some data on a tablet and looked up.

"Shit, man, you got fucked up," he said, looking at Moss's face. He tapped the screen. "Says here she's a wild one."

"Yeah, with a fucking robo hand," Moss complained.

"Don't worry. We'll break her of that right quick inside," the guard said and waved to a tower above.

"Looking forward to it," Moss said.

"Asshole," Ynna muttered under her breath and Moss didn't know if she meant him or the guard. His heart pounded, and his palms were numb. They had done some crazy missions, but this was something entirely new. They were giving themselves over to the very people who wanted them dead. They were ushered over to a parking spot, and Moss did his best to drive smoothly. He jerked to a spot once more, and he and Gibbs hopped out.

Looking around, Moss noticed few of the guards were wearing masks. They had driven through the misters beyond the walls, but that hardly seemed enough to stop the spread of some infection from engulfing the world. From everything he had heard and seen, he knew there was much more to be learned about the disease and, if he made it out of this alive, he wanted to find out what he could.

A guard approached, taking wide confident strides toward them. "Driver's training ain't what it used to be," she mocked. "You guys know the routine?"

"No, first day," Moss answered, very aware of his bruised and bloody face.

"Fresh meat?" she said, making no effort to hide her annoyance. "Can't believe we are so desperate that we have noobs doing transfers. Guess that's the age we live in. Well, each of you take one down to get processed and come back out here, and I'll get you sorted."

"Thank you," Gibbs said as he opened the side door of the transport.

"Thank you, *ma'am*," she emphasized.

He looked at her cautiously and parroted, "Thank you, ma'am."

"Not going to make this a long day for me, are you?" she questioned harshly.

"No, ma'am," Moss said as he unclipped Anders and made a show of dragging him from the vehicle.

"Good," she said, "just take them to that building there and see that they're washed and fitted."

She pointed to another square concrete building with the words "Guest Services," written above the door in block lettering. Moss pushed Anders forward, and Gibbs did the same with Ynna, who turned back to hiss over her shoulder.

"I guess you finally get to see me naked."

"Not exactly what I had in mind," Gibbs whispered.

"Your lucky day, too," Anders said to Moss.

"Dreams really do come true," Moss joked nervously. A

green light flashed on his wrist, and the metal door to the building slid open, leading to a bank of rooms with one-way glass windows looking in. He brought Anders into one of the small rooms, seeing the cameras pointing down at him. There was another door at the rear of the room which appeared to be stacked cinderblocks painted white. Metal nozzles protruded from the walls and ceiling, and a drain was set into the center of the floor.

The door closed behind them automatically, and Moss pressed a button on his wrist screen which opened the electronic locks which restrained the man. Moss scooped up the chains and shackles and turned to Anders, ordering, "strip," in as cold a voice as he could muster.

"Yes, sir," Anders said, playing the defeated man perfectly. As he pulled the one-piece jumpsuit from his body, Moss saw that his chiseled form was covered with poorly treated burns from his left calf all the way up part of his back. He wondered what kind of incident had done that to him.

Moss winced and turned to the locker sized machine in the corner of the room. Ynna had given them a vague sense of what to do, and he held his wrist toward the machine and selected PRINT UNIFORM.

The machine sent a beam into the room, which scanned Anders quickly before disappearing. Prisoners were not given their names, simply numbers based on their arrival date and time. The machine shook as it worked, and another gray and white striped jumpsuit fell into an open slot at the middle.

"Guest PM1005842022," was printed in bold letters across the chest. The machine rumbled again, and an electronically lockable collar dropped out. Moss lifted the collar and flipped it in his hands. Black leather with a single ring on the outside and electrodes that would press against the skin on the inside.

Moss had to work hard not to make a face at the appalling

device. He placed it back in the slot and slid closed a light plastic cover. He opened the door at the front of the room and stepped back into the hallway to join Gibbs, and they watched as their friends were blasted from all sides with icy water. They both had many things they wished to say at this moment but knew better as there was another guard in the hallway and more cameras watching their every move.

When the water shut off, the two were then blasted with powered air to dry off. It looked no more comfortable than the water. The guard watching from a chair in the corner of the hallway leered as Ynna dressed, one of his hands lost in the folds of his pants. Gibbs looked disgusted but did not speak. Moss was impressed that his friend was able to hold himself together through this and was unsure how Ynna and Anders would be after. At least Ynna had known what to expect, and Moss thought, given the little he knew about Anders and seeing the scars, he had probably been through worse.

Lights flashed next to the doors, and the two stepped back into the rooms, grabbing the wet clothes off the floor and swapping them out for the new ones. Moss gritted his teeth to keep from apologizing to Anders as he clipped the collar around his neck. One more tap of his wrist and Anders disappeared through the door at the rear of the room. The door closed and Moss turned, the easy part over. He walked over, and the two exited the building. The space between the walls was large and open with a few armed guards milling about. Industrial lights kept the space bright though everything was flat and dark. Parked trucks were off to one side with buildings on the other. The woman strode back over to them.

"All done?" she asked, and they nodded. "Good."

She looked to be in her late forties and walked with the proud, upright posture of someone who had possessed power for a long time. Her eyes were sharp and watched everything with judgmental exhaustion. Her armor appeared to be older but was kept in pristine condition, and she carried a baton rather than a gun at her hip. Moss wondered if she used that more on the guards than the prisoners.

"We've had a large influx the last two days, and your file shows your shift just started, so I'll get your training going now," she informed them. "If you have any questions, save them for the end because I'm going to tell you everything you need to know."

"Yes, ma'am," Moss and Gibbs said in unison.

"Good boys," she said as though she were speaking to dogs. "I take this job seriously, and I expect those beneath me to do the same. You'll be free to get the lay of the land, and I encourage you to walk the street and get a sense of the place. We don't take any guff from the guests, so if you see anything or if anyone says anything to you which you don't like, I expect it to be dealt with—no room for a soft touch in here.

"Don't make friends with the guests. Your job is to keep them in line. They try to get all buddy-buddy, they are trying to take advantage of you, remember that. You get three square meals in the employee mess which can be taken when you see fit, but don't dally. Your entry and exit are time-stamped, so I'll know if you are taking a long lunch. Same goes for sleep. You get seven hours in the barracks, but I expect you in uniform and on the streets after that time. This all making sense so far?"

"Yes, ma'am," they said once more as they passed through the bottom of a tower to the final wall. This was of strong stone and topped with spirals of barbed wire. The guard towers built into this wall had no doors and looked down onto the only passageway into the city—a massive programmable nanometal door which was caged in with electrified chain-link. She waved her wrist at a keypad, and the sound of arcing electricity fell silent. She opened the door with a key, and they stepped inside.

She turned the fencing back on before activating the door which shimmered into a liquid that opened a gap just large enough to walk through. They stepped beyond and were met by another electrified cage on the other side.

"Impressive," Gibbs observed, and the woman snorted.

"Unnecessary high-tech nonsense if you ask me," she said, "but the higher-ups say it deters the guests from trying to escape, so you'll hear no complaints from me. Escape prevention is your primary motivation day-to-day, so you need to keep your ears to the ground."

"Wouldn't that be easier if we can befriend the guests?" Gibbs asked, unable to help himself.

"Was some part of don't ask questions unclear to you?" the woman snarled.

"No, ma'am. Sorry, ma'am," Gibbs quickly apologized.

Her eyes narrowed as she stared into his face. "You want to make friends here?"

"No, ma'am," Gibbs stated, his body vibrating.

"Because it sounds like you do," she said.

"No, ma'am," Gibbs was nervous now. His inquisitive nature had no place in Carcer City. They stepped through the final gate and onto the pressed earth street surrounded on both sides by crudely constructed buildings.

"Guests who can afford materials are given the right to build here. They are under supervision the entire time and rent tools which are to be checked out and in by the supervising employee. Only managers can rent out the tool. Just as in the cities, managers have one stripe under the logo, senior managers have two and wardens have the garish flames," she said, tapping a gloved hand to her own emblem. "You will be assigned a quadrant every morning, of which there are four in the city. The guests can move freely between them during the day, curfew begins at twenty-one hundred, and everyone needs to be in their respective zones. You see a woman with the men or an aug with the pure, they will be moved. You understand?"

"Yes, ma'am," Moss said, the drying blood in his mouth guard making it difficult to speak. He wanted to get it off and wash his face but knew better than to show his face here. He knew he was not such a high value target that every Carcer employee would know his face, but he did not want to take any chances.

"I will take you now to meet your direct supervisor, Twelve, and he will see you settled in. Should you ever need to speak with me, I am Warden One of CC1 but ignoring the chain of command is a punishable offense, so I do not expect to see you again," she stated as they moved toward the imposing building at the center of the city. Red lines spray-painted onto the ground stretched from the structure, marking the separate quadrants. Prisoners moved away and spoke in hushed tones as they passed. A long, shrill scream emanated from down a street, and One turned to look. "Go inside and find Twelve," she snapped, turning robotically and marching toward the sound and away from them.

"We are in it now," Moss said cautiously.

"You think I should put on a fake voice?" Gibbs asked in an appalling English accent, "So we are harder to recognize."

"I think you're more likely to draw attention that way," Moss told him.

"Right," Gibbs said, disappointment in his voice.

"Listen, we have to stay real smart if we have any chance of surviving this," Moss warned.

"I know," Gibbs said. "How are we going to find the rest? Or your grandmother?"

"One problem at a time," Moss said. "We were lucky to make it this far, and it's only going to get more complicated. We are surrounded on all sides by people who would profit greatly if they figured us out, so we need to stay focused. We'll try to meet with Ynna and Anders tonight, but we have to get past this first." He pointed to the large building with a massive Carcer logo on the front.

"Belly of the beast," Gibbs said as they passed through fences and ascended the stairs. Just inside the building, a stocky man with little musculature under his armor looked up from the screen at his wrist.

"New guys?" he asked impatiently.

"Yes, sir," Moss answered in a fully subservient tone.

"One sent a message two minutes ago. What were you doing all that time, braiding each other's hair?" he asked aggressively.

Moss shifted uneasily. "No, sir."

"I know you weren't. You aren't ladies, are you?"

"No, sir," Moss said again, instantly despising the man.

"So, what were you doing?" Twelve barked.

"Getting the lay of the land, sir," Moss answered.

He snorted and faked a chuckle meant as mockery. "You need a survey team to go in a straight line?"

"No, sir. Sorry, sir," Moss said, and he realized how much they were going to have to change their style here.

"Silent plus-sized," he said, pointing to Gibbs (though Twelve was actually larger), "One says you want to make friends with the guests."

"No, sir," Gibbs murmured.

"No, you didn't say it, or no, you don't want to make friends with the guests?" he pressed, and a sheen of sweat broke out on Gibbs' forehead.

Gibbs swallowed hard and stuttered, "I don't want to make friends with the guests, sir."

"So, you are calling One a liar?" Twelve asked with affected confusion.

"Oh! No, sir," Gibbs exclaimed.

"So, you are calling me a liar?" Twelve's eyes opened wide with indignation.

"What? No. No, sir!" Gibbs said frantically, and Twelve blew his lips before letting out a loud false laugh.

"You new people are so easy to mess with." He chuckled to himself, though Moss felt as though all the air had been sucked from the large, open room. "Funny, right?" Twelve asked, and the two made nervous laughter. "You two are all right," he said and turned to guide them down a long hallway with rooms full of cots. They passed locker rooms and lounges with screens and beers for purchase to the end of the hall which opened into a large cafeteria.

"So, you've seen where you can sleep and rest for your mandated breaks, you boys hungry?" Twelve asked. Gibbs looked as though he was about to speak, so Moss piped up.

"No, sir. Hoping to get to work straight away," he said hurriedly. Gibbs' eyes looked forlorn, but he understood.

"I like that attitude," Twelve said with a suspicious smile. They breezed through the room to a door at the rear and exited back outside. The air was cool and heavy with fog. They moved beyond more fences, and Twelve turned to look at them. "Ready to see the real Carcer City?"

CHAPTER 15

The streets at the back of the building were different from those at the front. Large groups of men stood around, smoking and chatting. They didn't seem as concerned about the presence of the guards. Twelve scanned the people, disdain in his eyes. He started them walking down a street, and they took note of how crowded all the bars and restaurants were.

"You'll take the non-augmented men's quadrant tonight. I'll expect a report in the morning at end of shift," Twelve told them as he walked with an intentionally intimidating stride down the street. A young man hustled over from an alleyway.

"Manager Twelve," he panted.

"Yes?" Twelve said.

"We just removed two women from the quad," he said.

"Why was I not informed?" he barked.

"It happened so fast," the young man justified, though his nervousness was clear in his tone.

"Too fast to call me on comms?" Twelve pressed.

"Yes, sir. Well, no, sir. We just wanted to sort it for you," he stammered, and Twelve's eyes narrowed, and the corner of his mouth turned up slightly. Moss had known managers like this at

ThutoCo—people who had taken too much joy out of the discomfort of their employees. Mr. Greene had always mocked the type, saying their management got the worst out of those who worked for them. Thinking of him instantly brought the guilt back. Moss remembered the recording, and he wondered what had come of his old boss.

"Were you in the riots of seventy-nine?" Twelve asked.

"No, sir," the man said.

"I was," Twelve said with an air of superiority.

The man slumped his shoulders subserviently. "Yes, sir."

"You would not have survived," he stated coldly. "Begin your shift," he told Moss and Gibbs. "I need to follow up on this."

He puffed himself up and strode away.

"Hi, I'm Dimitry," the young man said with a genial little wave.

"Nice to meet you, Dimitry," Moss said, intentionally not introducing himself.

Dimitry asked, "You guys new?"

"First minutes," Moss admitted.

"Whoa," Dimitry said, "want a drink?"

Moss knew he shouldn't remove his mask around a stranger, but he was tired and overwhelmed, and a drink sounded perfect.

"Yes, please," Gibbs said, feeling the same way and sensing that the round-faced, freckled young man posed no threat to them. Dimitry guided them to a ramshackle structure constructed of ancient road signs soldered and bolted together. The words "pit stop" were cut out of scrap metal and affixed above the door. The smell of charred meat and beer filled their noses as they entered the room with prisoners sitting at crude tables cut of shipping boxes. No one even shot them a glance as they walked over the sticky floor to the bar. Dimitry held up three fingers and the tired, miserable-looking obese man behind the counter went about opening the beers slowly.

"How long have you been here?" Gibbs asked Dimitry, who shook his head.

"Three years," he informed them.

"And Twelve still talks to you like that?" Gibbs asked. Dimitry snorted a laugh.

"He talks to everyone like that," he said, "but you get used to it. Things are so crazy in here these days, and I hardly notice that kind of talk anymore."

"Why so crazy?" Moss asked.

"How hard was it for you to get this job?" Dimitry laughed.

Moss calculated his answer and tried to look calm as he peeled the respirator from his face, dried blood pulling at his skin. "Not hard," he guessed.

"Exactly!" Dimitry exclaimed. "Ever since the terrorist attack at ThutoCo, almost no one wants to work for the big companies. The turnover here is crazy. People are quitting left and right. There are as many managers as front-line guys like us."

Moss blanched. He had known the way the media painted what they had done but had never thought the public had bought it, yet this young man had called them, "Terrorists."

"You think they were terrorists?" Gibbs asked, pulling his own mask away. Moss was struck by the fact that they were revealing their faces while discussing their own actions with someone who thought them criminals.

"What else would you call them?" Dimitry asked as if it were the most obvious thing in the world. "They broke into a company, set off bombs, stole proprietary information, and killed a bunch of people." The bartender waddled over and set the beers before them, handing Moss a wet, dirty rag to wipe his face. Moss couldn't tell if the rag had been brown originally or if it had become that way over time, but he took it in the spirit it was intended and scrubbed at his mouth, wincing at the pain. "I got this round," Dimitry offered, tapping at the screen on his armor to make the payment. Moss made a note to check his own armor's balance when he had a chance.

"Didn't they know that ThutoCo was trying to kill their employees?" Gibbs offered lightly, taking a sip of the beer.

"What?" Dimitry scoffed. "If you believe that, I have a lake house to sell you! Problem is, a lot of people believe that bull and now we are desperate to keep staff."

"That is crazy," Moss echoed the youth's verbiage.

"Right?" he said.

"And your bosses don't care that you drink on shift?" Moss asked as he tipped his beer and took a sip.

"Nah, they run it pretty loose in here. For as much as it looks like a big-bad, and as hard as the bosses can be, no one cares too much as long as things aren't getting out of control," Dimitry explained cheerily.

"Sounded pretty strict about time management," Moss put in.

"Oh, sure," Dimitry agreed. "But when you're on shift, it's pretty loosy-goosy."

"Sounds like a pretty good job," Moss said, trying to keep the kid happy and talking.

"It is," Dimitry said and clinked his bottle against Moss's.

"The prisoners don't give you too hard a time?" Gibbs asked.

"The guests," Dimitry corrected, finishing his beer, "are good people for the most part. You have some people who are in here for violence and the like, but for the most part, it's just people who pissed off the wrong rich guy who could afford a bounty."

"I see," Moss said, feeling a sense of relief about the endeavor.

"I'll even tell you guys," Dimitry said in a hushed, conspiratorial tone. "I'm dating one of them."

Gibbs choked on his beer, the liquid foaming back into his bottle. "Really?"

"Yes," Dimitry said, clearly pleased with the reaction.

"And no one cares?" Moss asked.

"They would if they found out, but it's hard to get caught," he boasted.

"How's that?" Moss asked, hardly able to believe how forthright Dimitry was.

"The cameras are only on the streets and walls and are monitored by an AI that is on the lookout for unauthorized exits and the like," he said. "It would take an army of people on a round-the-clock schedule to watch all the feeds, so they farmed it out to computers. I have to piss," he informed them. "You guys want to get the next round?"

"Sure," Gibbs said, parading the menu on his screen as Dimitry stood and receded into the bar. The bartender had his broad back to them, but his ear was cocked.

"Reminds me of Sharon," Moss said, hoping Gibbs would pick up on the implication. Sharon had been an acquaintance of theirs at ThutoCo. A kind but awkward woman, Sharon had always shared too much information in the hopes of making friends. The tactic had never really worked as people always felt a certain level of distrust of her since they knew she was likely to repeat anything she had heard to the next person she came across.

Gibbs had used her style to mine her for information about girls he was interested in, and Moss hoped that he picked up on the fact that Moss wanted to keep this kid talking as long as they could. The information was vital if they had any hope of success.

"Agreed," Gibbs said, nodding slightly and Moss breathed a little easier in the knowledge that his friend understood. The bartender turned to look at them, bloodshot eyes scanning their faces.

"New?" he asked in a low, heavy voice.

"Yes," Moss said, "that obvious?"

The man snorted. "If there's anything you need, come by."

"What could we need?" Gibbs asked.

"I'm not saying anything. I'm just saying—if there is anything you need," he repeated cryptically, and Moss tapped his finger to his nose.

"Three beers for now," he said, and the man shifted away from them. Moss's eyes followed him down the space, and he turned to look around the bar. All the men sat either in silence or speaking quietly to one another. It struck him how different this place was from any of the other bars he had been to—there was no entertainment. In the city, everyone was plastered to one screen or another, and even at the Drudge's Head, there had been a performer. Here, there was nothing, just people sitting around drinking and talking.

Dimitry came back a moment later.

He smiled. "New beers, sweet. Thanks, fellas."

"No problem," Gibbs said. "Anything else we should know since it's our first day?"

"Not really," Dimitry said, downing more beer in another gulp.

"How do you keep the guests from exiting if the cameras do so little?" Gibbs asked.

"Just because they can't pick up a romance doesn't mean they don't do much. They look for quick movement and sparks and make a live map of everyone out on the streets which are monitored by supervisors," Dimitry said, sounding disinterested. The door opened, and Dimitry announced, "Here's my boyfriend now."

Moss's jaw nearly hit the floor as in walked the last person he expected to see and the only person who could ruin all their plans.

"This is Thomas," Dimitry said.

Moss watched as Mr. Greene's eyes went wide with recognition. His former boss had identified them instantly, and Moss knew the unfortunate man was in here because of his connection to them.

Mr. Greene could call it out, "Bring in the guards and have Moss arrested" on the spot. He considered pulling his weapon and making up an excuse later for his actions. He broke out in a sweat, his heart throbbed, and fear and guilt coursed through him. This could all have been for nothing.

But Mr. Greene walked over and played it cool.

"Dimy, you have new friends," he said, lacing his fingers through the young man's. Moss couldn't believe it. In addition to Mr, Greene not instantly raising alarms, he was happily married —the tan line still obvious from where his wedding band had been.

"You know, I don't remember your names," Dimitry said apologetically.

"I'm Marley, and this is Che," Gibbs offered a hand.

"Che, how appropriate," Mr. Greene said as he took Moss's hand.

He turned to Dimitry. "You know, sweetie, I was hoping to get you a little gift, and I think your new friend could help me with that. You think I could have a minute alone with this one?"

Moss had to give it to him. He was still clever.

"Sure," Dimitry beamed. "The pool room next to the bathroom is empty. I just saw."

"Thanks," Mr. Greene said happily, extracting his hands and hurrying toward the back. Moss shook like a leaf as he followed. He knew the older man had him over a barrel and could demand anything, but as they entered the room with a pool table held up with fused-together kegs, he turned and hugged Moss. "You alright?" he asked, and Moss could not speak. He was overcome with joy in the moment and gripped the man tight.

"Y—Yes," he stammered. "Are you? I'm so sorry for everything."

"Sorry?" Mr. Greene asked in his nasal voice.

"Yes, for all this, for everything you've been through. I saw the tape, I know they threatened you, and now you are here, and it's all my fault," Moss burst. Mr. Greene chuckled slightly.

"Sure, they threatened me and made me film that video, but I'm alive because of you. You exposed something which I had been suspecting for years, and I'll be forever grateful to you for that," he said, and his sincerity raised Moss up.

"But you're here," he insisted.

"I'm here because I began to rally people and help them break their contracts and get out. I was caught. A lot of people were caught, and most of us ended up here," he explained, a deep sadness in his tone. "Things have changed, bud. You changed the world."

"Not enough," Moss observed.

"Not yet," Mr. Greene agreed. "There is still work to do, but it looks like your Productivity Points are off the charts now."

Moss chuckled, and it was as if nothing had changed since that day in his office—Moss's last day at ThutoCo and the first day of his new life. "I think I may have hit Level 2," he quipped, and Mr. Greene smiled that inspiring smile which had gotten Moss through so much as a youth. "What's with you and the kid?"

"That was Brian's genius," he said of his husband. "He told me to get in with a guard so I would stay safe while he works to get me out of here. He's still on the board, but things are such a mess back at the company and suspicions are at an all-time high. It might be a while before he can free me, and I'm not tough enough to survive here without help."

"What about all the people from the company? You can't

form a little group? Watch out for each other?" Moss asked, hating what the man had to do to keep himself safe.

"We have," Mr. Greene told him, "but it's mostly pale engineers and managers who've never left the Burbs. It's not an intimidating presence. So, I made nice with the sap out there, and he makes sure no one bothers me. It was a smart plan, though I'm sick to my stomach at cheating."

"I'm sorry," Moss said, his guilt not assuaged.

"I'll survive," he said, "you're here for your grandmother?"

"Among other things," Moss said cryptically.

"Good," Mr. Greene encouraged. "I don't know how you'll do it," he paused, "but I don't know how you pulled off what you did."

"I work with some good people now," Moss told him.

"I'm happy to hear it," Mr. Greene replied, seeming genuinely happy for Moss. "You know she's being held in the VIP area. I don't know much, but I know it won't be easy. Low-level guards aren't allowed anywhere near it.

"Shit," Moss said, and Mr. Greene grimaced. "Sorry," Moss said, feeling as though he were back in the office about to be admonished.

"It's all right." Mr. Greene smiled. "I guess you've earned the right to swear."

"We could take you with us," Moss offered, "when we get out of here."

Mr. Greene pondered the offer for a moment, running his finger along a tear in the pool table's surface. "No," he said finally. "I want to walk out of here free."

"I understand," Moss said sadly.

"But I have observed enough in my time here to help you, I think," he offered before adding, "but I don't think we have too much more time now before the kid gets suspicious. He may be a rube, but he's jealous and insecure."

"Could you meet with us tomorrow at the Alco-Traz?" Moss asked.

"I haven't heard of it, but I'm sure I can make my way over," Mr. Greene agreed.

"Great," Moss said, "and Mr. Greene, it's great to see you, though I wish it were under different circumstances."

"You too, bud," Mr. Greene said as they embraced once more, "and you can call me Thomas."

"No, sir, I don't think I can," Moss admitted.

He smiled, truly happy to see his old mentor.

CHAPTER 16

After parting with Dimitry and Mr. Greene, Moss and Gibbs had made rounds, wandering the streets and acting like they were working while trying to get a sense of the place and its weaknesses. Once Dimitry had become drunk enough to answer more pointed questions without becoming suspicious, they had inquired after the Alco-Traz, and he had informed them it was on Seedy Street—so-called because it was both full of dive bars and it was where quadrants C and D met.

They had subsequently returned to the barracks and showered, eaten and rested. No one had batted an eye at the new recruits, and they had been careful to keep their faces covered as much as they could within reason. Moss's broken nose and swollen features helped to disguise him.

After what had amounted to a cat nap, they had another conversation with Twelve, equal parts awkward and condescending. Now they were back on the streets and ready to set their plans into motion.

They had expressed an interest in seeing more of the city, and Twelve had acquiesced, assigning them to D: augmented females. They had made their way to Seedy Street, but as it was early morning, the bars were mostly shuttered, so they set about looking for Ynna to no avail.

They had also gleaned one relevant piece of information overnight. While showering, an older woman had told them that breakouts were much more common than Carcer would like them to believe. "They have a system in place," she had told them. "See, when guests get out, they usually go to find their loved ones straight away. The friends or family are elated to see them and stop paying the guest rates. Carcer issues a bounty and picks up both the friend for defaulting on their payment and the escaped guest. Works more often than it doesn't, and Carcer doubles their profit."

Moss and Gibbs had acted astonished at the efficiency of the system while taking keen note of the fact that people had ways of getting out. In addition to now looking for their friends, they were also looking for someone who knew how to get out, though they knew that was decidedly unlikely dressed as they were.

"Officer!" The words broke them from their silence. A woman with half her face replaced with nanoskin came hustling over. The other half of her face was red with fury. She was gaunt, with green-dyed hair and a scared look just below the angry surface. "Officer!" she repeated, and Moss snapped to attention.

"Yes, ma'am?" he said, and she stopped dead in her tracks, seemingly surprised by his respectful response.

"That fat bitch juiced me!" she yelled, her ire back up.

"Pardon?" Gibbs asked, and Moss realized how truly ill-prepared they were. Carcer guards would have gone through extensive training and have protocols for all these types of incidents. Being cut loose and told to patrol as they were, they had no idea how to handle actual problems.

The woman huffed and began speaking in a patronizingly slow voice, stopping between every word, "That fat bitch juiced me." She pointed in the direction of a short, round, tough-looking woman with a crude robotic arm. She was standing with a group of other women, and she was swinging the arm around with pride.

"We'll have a chat with her," Moss offered.

"I know you will!" the woman insisted. They strode over to the group, trying their best to look intimidating.

"Excuse me," Moss said, and the woman stepped forward, obviously not scared by the two guards before her. From the stamp on her uniform, she had been there for over ten years and was not threatened by the new recruits.

"What?" she said in a thick accent.

"This guest says you stole her power," Moss informed her.

"And?" she said, crossing her arms, a light on the metal one flashing green.

"And is it true?" Moss asked, irritated with the entire situation. It had taken them longer than he had wanted even to get here and now that they were, he did not want to engage in petty squabbles when he could be out searching for his friends.

"No," she stated, and the women around her all snickered.

"We can check the vid," Gibbs reminded her.

"So, do it! Go away and check," she said, rolling her eyes to the great bemusement of her friends. Moss could feel his blood boiling.

"All right," Moss began, his tone serious and grim, "maybe I'll just take that fucking arm and juice her."

Gibbs seemed as shocked as the women and the green-haired woman hissed, "Yes!"

"Hey," Gibbs said, putting a hand on Moss's arm as he reached for his weapon.

"Listen to your friend," the woman said, still trying to sound tough through tremulous words.

"Give her back her fucking power," Moss seethed, not blinking, hardly breathing. His vision narrowed to her alone, and the world went quiet. The woman did not say anything in reply. She simply hung her head and flipped open a panel on her arm, pressing a few buttons. Moss watched as the light began to blink yellow, then red and the woman behind him gave a little cheer. Gibbs turned and shook his head to silence her enthusiasm.

"What do you say?" Moss growled, cold power in his words.

"W—what?" she stammered, looking up from her arm, sounding weak.

"What do you say?" Moss repeated.

"Sorry," the woman offered like a child caught doing something they shouldn't.

"Yeah, you fucking are!" the green-haired woman shouted.

"Get out of here!" Moss told her, and she moved away quickly. "And you," Moss turned back to the short woman, "don't pull this shit again. Life is hard enough in here without turning on each other."

"Sorry," she said with a hangdog look.

"What?" he snarled.

"Sorry, sir," she amended.

"Get out of here," he ordered, and the group dispersed, hurrying away down an alley. Moss turned to face the open plaza in which they were standing. People were beginning to push old carts on makeshift wheels into position. The space would become a bustling little market soon.

Gibbs looked at Moss and sighed. "Whoa."

"What?" Moss snapped, not having calmed down.

"That didn't take long," he said almost sheepishly.

Moss turned on him angrily. "What didn't?"

"You," Gibbs began, "to become like them."

Moss snorted. "Like who?"

"Nothing, forget it," Gibbs tried to drop it, taking a step away from Moss.

"No, like who?" Moss repeated, shaking his head and returning to himself.

"Like the other guards," he said in nearly a whisper.

Moss took a breath, calming down. "I'm not like them."

"All right," he said, sounding unconvinced.

"I'm not, it's just," he trailed off before continuing, "it's just hard enough without treating others this way. People shouldn't lose their humanity simply because they are in here."

"I agree," Gibbs said, and the implication was clear in his words.

They saw an elderly woman pushing a cart. The thin, gray hair stood out in patches against liver-spotted skin. Her frail body was hunched like a vulture as she shuffled slowly, straining under the weight of the cart. They went over to help her get set up.

"No," she said as they approached.

"We were hoping to help," Moss explained.

"No," she repeated, and as Moss was beginning to formulate a response, a yell cut through the air.

"Guard," a familiar voice screamed, and Moss and Gibbs turned at once. They saw Judy, covered in fresh bruises and welts helping a staggering Ynna who was pouring blood. They rushed over, and Gibbs scooped up Ynna and carried her over to a cement bench off to the side of the plaza.

"Ran into some old friends of hers," Judy explained. "I got her out of it, but she'll need some time."

"She needs a doctor," Moss stated as Gibbs tried to stem the bleeding from Ynna's nose.

Judy shook their head and stated plainly, "No, we don't need any extra attention."

"And you, how you holding up?" Moss worried.

"It's been a long few days, but they were mostly interested in how to get to you," Judy explained.

"I'm so sorry," Moss said.

"We all knew what we signed up for," Judy said, putting an arm on Moss's shoulder but retracting it quickly as they realized how it would appear to others.

"And you're okay so far in here?" Moss asked.

"You think it's the first time I've had to try and explain gray to dumbasses who know only black and white? It's been like this my whole life. I'll get a chance to teach them a thing or two. I actually think they were more pissed that one of their own had fallen in with criminals like you. I used to work for Carcer, remember?" they said with a smirk, and while he knew Judy was just trying to placate him, it worked.

"Still. I'm sorry," Moss said again. He hated the idea that his friends had all suffered worse because Carcer wanted information on him. He didn't understand why they were so desperate to have him more than any of the others.

"I know," Judy soothed, "but we've got a problem."

"Yeah, we're in a prison," Moss agreed.

"More than that," Judy told him, "she was recognized. If they realize it could be worth their while to tell Carcer who she really is, we're up a creek."

Moss moaned, wringing his hands. "Shit."

"Yeah," Judy agreed.

"Gibbs, you get her cleaned up, and to the bar, we have to sort something out," Moss said, and Gibbs gave a nod. He turned back to Judy, "You'll know them when you see them?"

"Yeah, but they won't be happy to see me," Judy reminded him.

"Because you just beat their asses?" Moss asked, and Judy raised an eyebrow. "Well, we can deal with that in the moment."

"Perhaps I'll just hang back," Judy offered as they guided Moss down a street of makeshift houses toward a wider structure of corrugated tin.

"Sure," Moss agreed. "Lucky it was us who you found."

"Luck had nothing to do with it," Judy corrected. "Ynna said you'd be waiting around here, so that's where I took her."

"Of course," Moss said, feeling foolish.

"And it wasn't luck that I found her either—I was waiting. I figured you guys would be dumb enough to pull something like this," they said.

"What choice did we have?" Moss asked, taken aback.

"Run, hide, save your skins, and start a new crew... it's what I would have done," Judy said, and though Moss chuckled awkwardly, he knew Judy wasn't kidding.

"I wasn't going to let you guys rot," Moss justified.

"And I'm grateful, don't get me wrong, but it's still stupid," Judy said and, as enemies surrounded them and they were about to deal with a potential threat, Moss had a hard time disagreeing. Judy pointed to a long, thin structure. Part of a billboard for fancy cocktails was tied with frayed rope to a frame and served as a door.

"Just inside there," Judy told him. "Two girls about Ynna's age. One with tattoos on her neck and the other with ripped sleeves. They will be licking their wounds and should be easy to spot. There are a lot of people in there, and you shouldn't expect a warm welcome."

"I'm getting used to that," Moss said with a weak smile.

"I'm sure." Judy laughed. "And stand up straight. You're supposed to be an authority figure, remember?"

Moss did as he was instructed, but the experience a moment earlier had taught him that he could be intimidating when he needed to be. Head held high, he strode into the building which seemed to be a community gathering center—old, torn couches wrapped in silver tape were set around industrial spools with board games etched into their faces. Screens were mounted in two corners, and while one flickered an old movie, the other was crisp, clearly showing a talk show where four people sat around discussing the issues of the day.

Along one wall was a bank of vidphones, of which about half were operable and occupied. Palmscreens, ocular implants, and lenscreens were shut off upon entering the city, meaning the only way to communicate with the outside world was to pay Carcer Corp for the luxury.

A bar stretched along the wall to the left, the chipper young girl working behind the counter pouring hearty amounts of brown liquor into mugs with coffee.

Everyone turned to face Moss as he walked through the door, though most went back to their conversations instantly. Though the room was mostly populated with women, there were a couple of men who had made their way over after curfew lifted.

Moss saw the two he was looking for standing in a corner. They were both fit and muscular, but he knew they must have jumped Ynna if they had been able to get one over on her. They did not look pleased to see that he was coming their way, but one of them masked it quickly.

"Hi, officer," she said in a sultry voice. She was not unattractive, quite the contrary, but Moss was not going to let this tack work on him.

He puffed himself up and spoke authoritatively. "Ma'am."

"Ma'am?" she repeated in affected dismay. "I think we're the same age."

"Ma'am, I heard you had an altercation with one of the other guests," Moss stated.

The other girl shifted, screwing her face into a grimace and trying to look hard. "Yeah, we dropped a bitch."

"Can't be doing that," Moss intoned.

"You might think differently if you knew who she was," the second girl said with a sibilant s. She had one bio-augmented eye which did not move as she spoke, simply sitting in the socket, pupil downcast.

"And who's that?" Moss asked, trying to play it cool though he knew how much trouble he was in. If they knew her and her connection to him, this whole operation would fail before it began. The girls scoffed. "What?" he asked.

"You think we are just going to tell you?" the second girl asked, all business.

"I think it would be best if you did," Moss said, raising his shoulders.

The first girl smiled, all honey and sweetness. "I think we are getting off on the wrong foot. I'm Whitney, and this is Astrid. We know someone in this facility is someone you might be interested in speaking with. Maybe there is a deal to be struck." While obviously scared and in pain from what Judy had done to her, she covered it with a light, effervescent tone.

Moss lowered his brows, "Are you trying to bribe an officer?"

Whitney clutched her hands to her heart in mock offense, "Absolutely not. I'm simply suggesting an exchange."

"What did you have in mind?" Moss asked, trying not to overplay his hand. He needed to keep them quiet but couldn't let them know it. Whitney batted her eyes at Moss, and her friend cringed.

"Well," she began, placing a bruised hand on Moss's chest plate, "pregnant girls get a discount on supplies in here, so maybe you could do a little something to me, and I can tell you something that will get you that promotion you want."

It took all his strength not to stagger back in shock. "What?" he said.

"I think you understand me," she said with a wink, flipping her hair over her shoulder before wincing at the movement.

"I do, it's just—" he stuttered, at a loss for words.

"It's just what?" Astrid said. "Only a man can demand sex in exchange for things?"

"Oh, what? No, I mean, it's just—" he was floundering and knew it.

"He's a shy one," Whitney joked to Astrid.

"What is it just?" Astrid pressed, looking him square in the eyes. He was flummoxed, and his heart was racing. He took a deep breath through his mask and regained his composure.

"It's just that I don't know if what you are saying is true. You could simply be desperate because of your situation and be looking to take advantage," he mustered.

"We aren't," Astrid put plainly, and he would have believed her even if he didn't already know she was telling the truth. He tried to work out some other arrangement in his mind. He wasn't going to whore himself and was certainly not going to father a child with this woman just to get them out of a jam. He considered taking them in, bringing them to solitary confinement and leaving them, but he knew they would make this offer to someone else and that eventually, a guard would likely take it.

He stalled for time, "Can you prove it? Give me some way of knowing what you are offering is legit?"

Astrid looked to her friend, who was now tracing lines with her fingertips on Moss's arm. "What we can tell you is that we used to run with her on the outside and know who she runs with now. We've seen the news," and she paused to give weight to what she added, "and even digitally distorted, we know she is valuable."

"What's to stop me from just watching the footage and finding out who you got into the fight with?" Moss asked, playing his part while he tried to come up with an offer. Whitney's hands were moving over him more aggressively, and he needed to think fast, a cold sweat breaking out on his skin.

"You could, but that would take time we could use to have

this chat with one of your coworkers," Whitney said, cocking her head suggestively.

Moss looked at Astrid, her robotic eye limp as her other was fixed on Moss. He smiled. "What if I could offer you something better, would that give me exclusive rights to your information?"

"What's better?" Astrid asked.

"Power," Moss said, proud of himself.

"We are already pretty tough," Astrid informed him.

"Not that kind of power, electricity," Moss explained. "You're both augmented, right? What if I got you a supply of power, as much as you could use, would that work?" Astrid's eye lit up. Moss had seen remote batteries in the barracks for augmented guards to use while on shift.

"That could work," Astrid said.

Whitney snorted. "My augments are broken anyway."

"I could help you with that, too," Moss told her.

"We have to talk," Astrid said, pulling Whitney by the arm so they could confer in private. Moss beamed. His plan might work. They spoke in hushed tones a few feet away while he absently watched the scene in the corner. They returned to his side after a time, Astrid looking excited while Whitney appeared disappointed.

"We'll do it," Astrid said, extending a hand and Moss exhaled for what felt like the first time in days.

CHAPTER 17

Moss and Judy entered the Alco-Traz, having worked out their deal with the girls. After taking time to convince them to allow Judy to work on them, Moss had rushed back to the barracks and returned to charge them. They had promised not to tell anyone else about Ynna, and while he didn't entirely trust them, it would do for the time being.

As they entered, they saw Mr, Greene speaking with Gibbs, Ynna, and Stan (who looked as though he had been more aggressively questioned than Judy—bruises, cuts, and burns peppering his body). He stood instantly as they entered and embraced Judy in a massive, one-armed hug. Ynna looked bored but seemed to be healing, and Gibbs was enthralled, hardly acknowledging Moss and asking, "What is the Peter Principal?"

Mr. Greene smiled broadly as Moss sat down at the round table. "Ah, that's the question," Mr. Greene said. "The principal posits that people are promoted to their level of incompetence. A person may be a great salesman but find that they are not good at managing other salesmen once they are promoted." Moss smiled. He had always loved listening to Mr. Greene philosophize about business. When he was younger, he would sit in the older man's office and simply let him speak. It also made him happy that Gibbs seemed to be enjoying it as well.

Mr. Greene continued, "It's why ThutoCo was always so successful. We used a system of promotion which incorporated skills beyond the actual job a person was doing, and it's why you might have some luck here. Carcer is so top-heavy with petty tyrants that the average employee can get away with anything."

"I just did," Moss said, thinking about how easy it had been to get the battery he had needed.

Gibbs only then seemed to notice Moss and asked, "Sort everything out?"

"For now," Moss told him. Gibbs looked relieved.

Moss felt a massive hand on his back. He stood to embrace Stan, his arm pulling Moss in tight.

"How you holding up?" Moss asked.

Stan looked at him with a weak smile. "Been better."

Moss smiled back. "That's the prevailing opinion."

"You're working on a plan?" Stan asked.

Moss sighed. "Still getting a sense of the place. Feels like I've been playing catch-up since you guys were taken. Any idea how they found you?"

Stan shook his head, "No."

"You give them anything?" Moss asked, wanting to make sure he knew everything which Carcer did.

"Would I look like this if I did?" he said, spreading his arm to highlight his wounds. A long streak of blood was drying along his chest. Judy stood behind him defensively, like a snake ready to strike. He continued, "They seem real interested in you."

"Any of you plan to order anything?" the bartender asked aggressively.

Not wanting to draw more attention to the table full of guards and inmates sitting together as friends, Gibbs stood and walked over to the bar and began ordering.

"You seen Patchwork?" Moss asked, worried for the youngest member of their team.

"Nah, I know he was trying to wipe his data, but they may be trying to break into him," Stan suggested.

"Poor kid," Moss said, hanging his head pitifully.

"Tougher than he looks," Judy pointed out.

"What's the plan?" Stan asked. He had told Moss that he sometimes liked to push people by letting them push themselves. Moss had always been so grateful for Stan's help and guidance, but right now, he really wished Stan would just give him a moment to think.

He shifted nervously. "Get my grandmother out of the VIP area and then escape."

"Oh, good." Stan chuckled. "For a moment, I was worried your plan would be vague."

Moss let out a long breath. "We'll figure something out."

"I appreciate you guys coming for us," Stan added, and Moss shot a look at Judy.

Judy gave him a flat look. "It's not news to anyone that he's nicer than I am."

"I might be able to help," Mr. Greene put in.

"And who are you?" Judy asked, folding their arms.

"Moss used to work for me at ThutoCo," Mr. Greene stated.

"Great, another fucking bub," Judy said with an eye roll.

Mr. Greene rapped a finger to his temple and smirked, "A smart fucking bub."

"What do you have for us, then?" Judy pressed.

"As I was saying, this is a backward company which has few front-line staff, and those which they do have are overworked, underpaid, and angry. I've seen enough corporate malcontents to know trouble when I see it. I don't think it would take much to push them over the line," he explained.

"Wouldn't the sheer number of managers be able to stop an angry mob of staff?" Moss asked thoughtfully.

"You would think that, but the company is fractured. With so many bosses all vying for attention, praise, and bonuses, they don't communicate with one another. They spend their time micromanaging their staff. In time, they would certainly be able to quell an in-house rebellion, but as I said, it would take time," he explained as Gibbs returned with metal cups of coffee, clanking them on the table.

"Twelve does seem more interested in belittling us than doing a job," Gibbs noted.

"Precisely," Mr. Greene said, taking a warm cup in his hand and taking a sip before wincing at the taste. He croaked, "Thank you."

"So, if we get the guards pissed, maybe it will buy us the time to get my grandma out," Moss offered and was met with nods.

"If you all work on the guests, we could really set this place ablaze," Mr. Greene added.

Stan smirked and hooked a thumb at Mr. Greene. "I like this one."

Mr. Greene responded with a bow of his head. "I try."

Stan winked. "And, Moss, for future reference, *that* is a plan."

Moss ignored the comment. "What do you know about the VIP area?"

"Not as much as I would like," Mr. Greene said, stroking his beard. The facial hair which had always been so pristinely trimmed was now a tangled mess. "I know it is located by the northwest side of the city and surveilled by a special, central control tower. I've only ever seen higher ranking people entering and exiting, so you will need clearance."

"Or better yet, someone in the control room," Moss said. "We will need the comms to speak with the outside world. We have Anders' van, but we will need support."

"Who's Anders?" Stan asked.

"A space pirate," Gibbs said, his derision clear in his voice.

"A friend," Moss corrected.

Ynna cleared her throat. "He got us here and helped us get in," she said, her voice hoarse.

"We will need to find him and Patchwork if we are going to have any hope of succeeding," Moss said.

"Anyone's guess as to how long they will keep Patch," Stan pointed out.

"Once he is back with us, we'll need to get him to that control room to get this ball rolling," Moss said.

Stan smirked. "What's the plan?"

"Right. Gibbs and I will start getting the guards pissed, and you guys do the same out here. We will meet here every morning to discuss progress. When the time is right, we will light our fuses and, in the chaos, break my grandma out and go," Moss said with surety.

"You know we will probably all be killed," Judy said with an amused smile.

"What else is new? But we made it this far," Ynna pointed out.

"You have me there," Judy said, pretending to tip a hat.

"We have to get back to the barracks to check in, but we'll see you guys tomorrow. Keep your eyes and ears open for anything that will help us," Moss said and stood. Gibbs did as well, putting a hand on Ynna's shoulder and giving a little squeeze.

As they moved toward the door, Moss felt a tug at his wrist and turned around.

"Moss," Mr. Greene said, his clear eyes fixed on his old protégé. "I just wanted to say that seeing you just now made me truly realize that you have become the man I always hoped you would. I'm proud of you."

Moss nearly collapsed to the floor, overcome with gratitude for the words. "Thank you," he mustered and extended a hand.

Mr. Greene shook it.

MOSS KNELT, fumbling with the battery, trying to angle it just right into the charging station when he heard footfalls approaching from behind.

"New guy," he heard Twelve's voice say.

Moss worked to get the battery in, but it was even more difficult with someone watching. "Just give me a second."

"One," the warden counted. "That was one second."

"I didn't mean—" Moss said, his hands beginning to shake.

"Didn't mean what you said?" Twelve pressed, looming over Moss, boots entering his field of vision.

"It's an expression," Moss hissed. He knew he had to humor his boss, but he was in no mood for it. His hand vibrated with ire.

"*You* said one second, not me," Twelve said, superiority hanging on every word.

"I know you didn't," Moss said, utterly perplexed by the aggressive stupidity of the man. He jammed the battery in and stood to face Twelve.

"So, now you are putting words in my mouth?" Twelve said, stepping closer. He was centimeters from Moss's face, his hot, sour breath hanging between them.

"What? No. What?" Moss stuttered.

"You said, 'one second.' Those were the exact words, and I gave you one second, and now you are arguing with me?" he snarled. Moss didn't know what to say. There seemed to be no answer which made sense. He hoped Twelve would play it off as though he was joking again, but he seemed to be in a bad mood.

Moss knew what the man needed to hear. "Sorry, sir."

"That's right," Twelve said. He stood with balled fists on his hips.

"What can I do for you, sir?" Moss asked. He tried to make himself small so the man would feel more powerful. It seemed to work.

"Update," Twelve demanded.

"Resolved a fight, sir. Other than that, all quiet," Moss informed him.

"A fight? And you didn't inform me?" Twelve said with a threatening tone.

"It was small, sir, not worthy of your time, busy and important as you are," he flattered and hung his head. Much as it pained him, playing the sycophant seemed to work best.

"I'll decide what's important. But you are right that I am busy. I expect a full report," Twelve said.

Moss nodded vigorously. "You will have it."

"Good," Twelve said, looking Moss over. "What were you doing with that battery?"

Moss stiffened. "They are for my legs, sir."

Twelve snorted. "You know you can charge in your room?"

"Oh, thank you, sir," Moss said. Twelve eyed him suspiciously.

"Something you want to tell me?" Twelve asked. Moss could tell the man was taking a shot in the dark, but he didn't want him to grow more interested. He calculated what answer would get the man off his back.

"No, sir. Just happy to be aboard," he said, wearing a false smile. The man nodded his approval.

"Good. Get back to work," he said and stomped off. Moss sighed. He knew Twelve's suspicious nature could cause problems if he wasn't careful. He went and gathered Gibbs from the bathroom, and they made their way to the mess hall.

"Just ran into Twelve, fucking prick," Moss said.

Gibbs turned with an eyebrow raised. "He suspect anything?"

"No," Moss said, "but we need to be careful with him."

"But Thomas said," Gibbs began, and Moss held up a hand to stop him.

"I know what he said, but Twelve is like a dog without a bone, and if we give him anything, he'll latch onto our asses so quick we won't be able to get anything done here," Moss said.

Gibbs nodded as they entered the mess hall. Rows of plastic tables were set under fluorescent lights, the room glowing bright white. As Carcer didn't trust drudges, human guards were tasked with keeping the place clean and serving the food.

They waited in line, shoes squeaking on the floor as they shuffled forward. Everyone picked up trays and plates as they went and were served a warm lumpy porridge which smelled like medicine. Gibbs grimaced at the food as Moss surveyed the room.

"What now?" Gibbs asked, holding his tray with one hand and poking the gray substance with a spoon. It jiggled slightly, and Gibbs moaned.

"Now we make friends," Moss said and lifted his head in the direction of a table of young bruisers.

Gibbs looked and sighed. "Why not start with those old-timers," he said, pointing a spoon, the affixed blob of food hardly moving.

"No," Moss said. "The folks who have been here a while won't want to hear what a couple of kids have to say. They've been at this too long, and while I'm sure they have more reasons to be pissed than anyone if they are still here, they are lifers."

"Smart," Gibbs said.

"We will get the other new people on our side first and work on the veterans once there are more of us," Moss explained. He led Gibbs to the table where the young people were all sitting around, joking and laughing.

"Mind if we join?" Gibbs asked, not setting his tray until they agreed.

A young, immensely muscular woman looked up at them. Her head was shaved clean, glistening in the bright light, and a scar bisected her face. Her cybernetic ears tilted and moved, the metal dishes shifting to face them. She smiled amiably, but Moss could tell she wasn't enthusiastic about the intrusion. "Sure," she said and gestured for the two men opposite her to scooch over.

"You two new?" she asked to fill the void.

"Yeah," Gibbs said, setting his tray down with a bang.

"How you finding it?" she asked. Moss found it interesting that she had invited them to sit on the side opposite her when there was plenty of space on the bench next to her. With all of them gathered opposite, it was as if she was holding court. He knew she would be the one to get riled up.

"So far, so good," Gibbs said with a smile. "The food leaves a little bit to be desired."

She laughed. "You get used to it."

"Doubt it," Gibbs said without missing a beat.

"I'm Dan, and these two are Kevin and Kyle, but everyone just calls them the Ks since they are always together," she said and pointed to the two strong, pale men with flat top blond hair. Moss made a note that Kevin had brown eyes and Kyle blue so he could tell them apart later. He wanted to be sure to play nice.

"How long you guys been here?" Moss asked.

The Ks did not answer. "A few years," Dan said, scooping a large spoonful of the porridge into her mouth and chewing loudly.

"What should we know?" Moss asked, not wanting to get ahead of himself.

"It's a tough job, but you have to be tougher," Dan said, the gray mush moving in her mouth as she spoke. "The guests mostly do their own thing, but you have to be vigilant. Let your guard down, and they will be quick to take advantage."

"And the bosses?" Gibbs asked and took a spoonful before making a sound of disgust which the Ks chuckled at.

"Bosses will ride your ass since they don't have much else to do," Dan said, turning her big, dark eyes on them. "Just keep your heads down and make it through the days."

Moss saw his opening, "And just wait for payday?"

Dan made a sound of annoyance with the back of her throat. "Right."

"What?" Moss asked, happy he had hit the nerve he had hoped to. He had worried he was rushing it but figured that disgruntled folks might be keen to share their grievances.

She looked at them with pity. "You guys that new?"

"Pretty new," Gibbs said.

"Well, let me fill you in on a little something. Our pay here is supposed to be automated but," and here she used air quotes with her fingers, "the system is down."

Moss played at being surprised. "We don't get paid?"

"Oh, we get paid," she said, "but it's often late, or the wrong amount or bonus you earned hasn't been filed yet. There is always some nonsense. Some bullshit which keeps your family hungry and you from being able to quit."

"Well, that sucks," Gibbs groused. He played disgruntled perfectly.

"It does," the Ks agreed as one. Moss was surprised by the uniformity of the way they spoke. He looked down, finally deciding to try the meal. He was shocked that despite its strong odor, it tasted like nothing. A gray blob which had as much flavor as it did appearance. Posters hung around the room, lauding the nutritional value of the "specially formulated diet," but Moss laughed that they forgot about taste.

He had meant to ask Gibbs about the posters which lined the walls. His friend had always considered himself quite the poster aficionado, and Moss wondered what he thought about all the ones here which promoted service to the company.

He gulped down the bite and looked at Dan. "Is there anything we can do about our pay?"

"We've tried, but they don't listen. They hold all the cards," Dan said miserably.

"Do they?" Moss asked, letting an implicit tone say more than his words.

Dan seemed unimpressed, "They do."

Moss decided he would get the ball rolling, even if just in a small way. He had time to get people motivated, but he needed to start laying the foundation. "We used to work for BurbSec at ThutoCo, and you may have heard some things changed there recently. That was all because of the little people," he said and scooped some more food into his mouth.

Dan smiled genuinely for the first time since they sat down. "I'm listening."

PART III

CHAPTER 18

The next week was spent sowing more seeds of anger around the facility. While Moss and Gibbs worked on the guards, the rest worked on the inmates. Anders had appeared on the second morning and was doing his part to help. Moss appreciated all the man had done for relative strangers though Gibbs continued to look on him with annoyance.

Doing recon on the city, they had learned more about the VIP area. Set into one corner, it was built atop an old factory and could only be reached by a single staircase which ran alongside the control tower. Drones and cameras watched the whole city, but this area had around-the-clock, intensive surveillance. As Mr. Greene had informed them, only managers were allowed in, bringing food and supplies to the hovels separated by electrified chain-link. Moss had figured that once they began getting the guards riled up, he could break in but needed to get someone with computer skills into the tower. Ynna said she could be helpful, but if they wanted to do it quickly, they needed Patchwork.

AS THEY ALL sat around in the turn of the century themed bar, a frail shape shadowed the door and collapsed to the floor. They all rushed and saw Patchwork, gaunt, and beaten. His eyes were swollen shut with blood, and he looked as though he had not eaten for days. They rushed to his side and pulled a few chairs together so he could lay down. Ynna ordered him some toast and brought a cup of water over, letting him sip at it slowly.

"Jo is gonna kick my ass," Ynna half-joked.

"You are not wrong," Moss said, looking with sorrow at the abused body of his friend.

"Probably kick Burn's body's ass while she's at it," Ynna said. Patchwork gave a weak smile, and Moss was happy to know he could hear them.

"Patch, you're with us now," he said, and the young man tried to open his eyes but couldn't. Blood coated his face from where they had pulled strands of dreadlock from his scalp.

"Monsters," Mr. Greene said, looking at what they had done to him.

Stan cracked his knuckles against his hip bone. "They haven't met us yet."

Moss knew that tone and turned to try and calm Stan down, but Judy was already on it, placing a hand on the massive man's chest and getting on their toes to whisper in his ear. Looking at Patchwork lying there, Moss was also enraged. He wanted to take down Carcer, destroy their allies in the AIC who controlled everyone's life and free the world from the yoke of the corporations. He knew his grandmother would help them with that, and he needed to free her and get his friends clear of this place. He felt his body begin to shake but took a deep breath to calm himself.

After a while, Patchwork finally spoke. "They got nothing," he wheezed in a whisper.

"That's great," Ynna told him, kneeling at his side and placing a hand on his chest.

"Good job, Patch," Moss added. He was proud of the young man and could not even imagine what he had endured to keep their secrets.

"I told them I had wiped," Patchwork said. "I told them."

"It's okay," Ynna whimpered. Moss had never seen her like this. Even when she had been shot and thought she was going to die, she remained tough and determined, but seeing her friend like this appeared to be breaking her.

"Moss," Patchwork said so quietly that Moss had to lean in. He took the young man's hand in his.

"Yes?" he asked, not caring how it appeared that a guard was holding a prisoner.

"They want you," he said. A chill went down his spine. He had known it, everyone had told him as they came out, but this was different.

"I know, I know," Moss stuttered, his heart breaking. All these people had been through so much to keep him safe from Carcer. It was almost too much to bear.

"Why?" Patchwork asked the question which Moss himself had been considering nearly every moment.

"I don't know," he admitted. He offered the one answer which made the most sense to him. "ThutoCo must have one hell of a bounty on me."

"Seems like more than that," Judy stated.

Stan nodded. "They want you for something. They kept asking, kept pressing. Like my information didn't matter unless it led to you. You have something they want."

Moss stood, scratching at his neck as he considered the words. "They don't know the program my father gave me was destroyed. Maybe they want that? Maybe they think I still have a way to break their systems?"

"That sounds right," Patchwork grumbled and turned his head to the side to allow Ynna to give him more water.

"Moss, if they figure out who you are," Mr. Greene began, but Moss interrupted.

"I know, I know," he said. He didn't want to think about that too much. The week had been nerve-wracking enough. It had been easy to get the other guards to consider making trouble, but every conversation he had made him nervous. He would constantly look over his shoulder, expecting someone to be listening. He worried that he would try to get the wrong person involved and they would turn him in. It was a high-risk gambit, and it only made matters worse that they so desperately wanted to find him.

Perspiration beaded on his forehead and he pulled Ynna aside. "Still no word from Grimy?"

She shook her head.

"Any idea how long it will take Patch to recover?" he asked.

"Not really my area of expertise." She shrugged. "I know he'll need longer than we can give him. Things are working out here. Turns out that a city full of prisoners is not a difficult place to motivate a group into rioting—shock of shocks. It actually feels like we almost have to hold them back."

Moss smirked. "Right. The guards, too. We are closing in on a tipping point."

"But he'll need time. Shit, man, he can't even open his eyes. Plus they'll have shut down any hardware in his head. Judy will need to work on him and who's to say when he'll be in fighting form," Ynna explained, tucking her hair behind an ear.

"In a pinch, maybe he could talk you through it?" Moss asked hopefully.

Ynna considered it for a moment. "Maybe, but you'll need me out there. Better to have Gibbs watch his back so I can cover Judy while they hotwire us a van."

"Yeah," Moss agreed. "This situation is getting really fucking complicated."

"In news to no one," Ynna mocked.

THE DOOR to the bar slammed open.

"What. Is. This?" a familiar voice demanded. Moss didn't even have to turn to know it was Twelve. He darted over quickly and stood at rigid attention. Gibbs was by his side a moment later.

"Sir," Moss acknowledged.

"Looks like One was right that you two just want to make friends," he said, pointing a finger, the accusation clear in his tone.

Judy hurried from the bar.

"No, sir," Gibbs said.

Moss jumped in before Twelve could send them spiraling into a semantic game. "This guest was injured," Moss pointed to Patchwork, "and we were making sure these others were staying calm and not trying anything funny."

Twelve's eyes narrowed. "You think I'm stupid?"

"No, sir," Moss said, keeping his body at attention though his hand shifted slowly toward his sidearm.

"And you," he said, turning to face Gibbs, "you think I'm stupid?"

Gibbs' face was red, and he was visibly shaking. Moss knew that while it made them appear guilty, fear was what Twelve wanted to inspire and Gibbs nerves might actually keep them safe.

"No, sir," Gibbs forced from his lips. "Why, sir?"

"Why?" Twelve mocked. "I was told one thing about you, and now I see this. What am I supposed to think?"

Questions like this from Twelve kept tripping Moss up, and he worked to figure out the answer the man wanted to hear. The rest of the crew busied themselves behind him, watching for any sign of trouble. Moss knew that they weren't ready, though. He knew he couldn't start anything just yet. He needed to buy them more time.

"Well," he began, trying to find the words.

The radio in Twelve's helmet crackled and, at that moment, Moss loved Judy more than anyone on the earth. Twelve pressed two fingers to the side of his helmet to hear, and his eyes shifted.

"We have a situation," he informed them gruffly. "Follow me. We'll see where your loyalties lie."

Moss and Gibbs followed him out on to the street without saying a word. He guided them through the people in their matching striped outfits. They cleared the way as the three passed, but they watched with interest to see where they might be going in such a hurry. Some even followed, keeping enough distance in an attempt not to be noticed. Judy hurried in the other direction, giving a slight nod to Moss as they passed.

As they rounded a corner, they saw what amounted to a brawl. Drones buzzed overhead, and two guards stood off to the side, watching the action unfold with bemused expressions on their faces.

Twelve rushed over to the other guards as five inmates pummeled one another. Two held one down as two more tussled on the dirt.

Moss turned to Gibbs. "You need to crack a skull," he ordered.

Gibbs blanched. "But—" he began.

"No," Moss hissed. "You have to. We need to get him off the scent, and Judy just gave us an opening. You have to."

Moss watched as his friend looked to the ground, forlorn. Gibbs gritted his teeth. "All right."

They moved over to where the guards were conferring. As they approached, Moss realized it was the Ks under the black armor.

"You four, deal with this," Twelve commanded. Moss laughed to himself that of course, Twelve did not seem to have any intention of helping them.

"You two, take the scrum, we'll take these," Moss commanded and moved toward the two still thrashing on the ground. He heaved the man on top up and threw him to the ground.

Since leaving ThutoCo, both he and Gibbs had been working out and learning to fight. Moss had taken to it much more naturally than his friend, but they were both strong and knew what they were doing.

Gibbs pounced on the man already on the ground and pulled his weapon, striking the man on the head with the metal butt of his pistol. The man let out a cry, and Gibbs looked just as pained as his victim. Moss loomed over the man he had thrown and ordered, "Hands behind your back."

The Ks were making short work of the other three, pummeling them until they, too, lay on the ground awaiting restraint. More guards appeared from every direction, shackling the fighters and dragging them away. The inmates had ceased their thrashing and seemed resolved to their fate as they were ushered quickly away. Gibbs put on a hard face which looked ridiculous to Moss but which seemed to have the desired effect on Twelve.

"That's what I like to see," he said, striding over to them with his thumbs hooked in his belt.

Gibbs nodded and made his voice several octaves lower than normal. "Yes, sir."

"I'll—" began Twelve.

The Ks chimed in, "A full report."

"Right," Twelve said. "Good men."

His last comment sounded to Moss like a dog owner

commending his pet. Twelve skulked away after the cadre of guards down the street.

"Piece of garbage," Kyle said.

"Piece of shit," Kevin corrected, raising an eyebrow.

"He's going to be in for a rude awakening," Kyle added with an obscene gesture.

Kevin let a devilish grin cross his face as he balled one hand into his fist theatrically. "They all are."

"We are ready to march, most of the fellas want in," Kyle told Moss. He had a crazed look in his eye. "Dan has everyone ready."

"Good," Moss said in an authoritative tone. "We will be ready soon, and we can finally have our voices heard."

"That we will," Kyle said and clapped Moss on the shoulder. Moss smiled and played at punching him in the stomach. Kyle reeled as though a bullet had struck him and fell to the ground, crying out, "My life!"

Kevin chuckled along before asking, "See you guys for dinner?"

"You know it," Moss said, lifting his fists and shimmying his shoulders in mock boxing moves.

Kevin lifted his hands defensively and wailed, "Not me, too!"

He picked his friend up off the ground, and they strode away, laughing.

Moss turned to Gibbs. He was not laughing. He looked miserable and angry, wearing an expression Moss had only seen a few times in his life.

"You all right?" Moss asked, giving his friend a chance to air his grievances more than actually asking.

Gibbs brows lowered, and his head shook. "No, I'm not fu— no, I'm not all right. What are we doing here?"

"Helping our friends," Moss tried to reassure him, but he

knew the words sounded hollow. Gibbs was in pain, and he just wanted to help but was unsure what he needed.

"I know, but Moss... what we are doing. What we have to do, it's all so much," he said, his voice quivering.

"It is, but you're doing great," Moss said.

"Am I?" Gibbs shrieked, throwing his hands up. Moss looked around to make sure no one was watching them. Most of the rubberneckers had moved on, but he ushered Gibbs into a side alley with a hand on his back.

"Gibbs, listen to me. Our friends needed us, and we are doing what needs to be done to free them. I know how hard this has been for you and I know you have had to do difficult things, but you've proven how strong you are. I couldn't have done any of this without you. We just have to stay strong a little while longer, and we can get out of here," Moss said.

Leaving the Burb for this life would have been brutal for Moss but having his friend by his side had made it possible to keep going. He wanted to give his friend the strength he so often gave Moss. He wanted to say something more, but he waited.

Gibbs took a deep breath and hung his head. "Thank you. It just feels like we are hurting so many people to help our friends."

"We are," Moss admitted, trying to shake the memory of what he had done outside the walls of Carcer City.

"I just hit a man who was only in a fight because of us," Gibbs said, his sorrow returning.

"If Judy got them riled up that easily, they wanted a fight," Moss pointed out.

"I suppose," Gibbs admitted.

"Just a little bit longer and we will be able to get our plan going," Moss assured him.

"That's it, too—our plan. What we are going to do. It's going to hurt people. The Ks have been friends to us in our role as new guards. They could die helping us do something they have no idea we are doing," Gibbs said. It was clear to Moss that Gibbs needed to get all his points out of his system.

Moss thought about what he had said. "The thing is, we are doing right by them, too. Sure, our motivations are not what we claim, but the guards here are as much prisoners as the inmates. This company holds their pay hostage so they can never leave, and they should demand to be heard. They want to do this with us not for our friends but for themselves, and we are actually doing some good."

Gibbs nodded, listening to Moss's words carefully. He seemed to have calmed down. "That is true," he admitted.

Moss put a hand on his friend's shoulder. "Gibbs, I'm glad you're with me."

Gibbs smiled so broadly he looked as though he was going to burst. "Always. Now, let's start a revolution."

CHAPTER 19

Patchwork's recovery was slow, and Moss was becoming increasingly nervous that they had not heard from Grimy. Things on both sides were reaching a fever pitch—the guards were ready to demand pay, and the inmates were ready to riot.

Moss was strapping on his gear in a small sleeping room when he felt someone come around the small privacy wall.

"Moss," he heard the familiar voice hiss. He tried not to react, but his body twitched. Twelve let out a laugh as he pressed the barrel of his gun against Moss's neck. His worst fears had been realized. He had been caught before getting the chance to set his plan into motion.

"I knew there was more to you than you let on. You thought you could fool me, but I'm not so dumb," Twelve bragged.

Moss turned around slowly with his hands raised. He was surprised to see that Twelve had come alone, but quickly remembered what Mr. Greene had said about managers jockeying for position within the company. As he shifted to see around the wall, he noted that the barracks were also empty.

Twelve grinned like a shark. "You are one of the most valuable assets in the world, did you know that?"

Moss was not surprised that Twelve wanted to revel in the moment. A man who trafficked in intimidation, bullying, and smug self-satisfaction would need to boast.

"Well, I'm pretty great," Moss said with a smirk, analyzing the situation. Twelve was burly, but the years of ordering others to do his work had made him soft and slow. The gun leveled at Moss's head was intimidating, but Moss was fast and tough. He had to bide his time and wait for his opening. "So, how did you figure it out?"

Twelve's grin grew wider. "Trying to get me to talk won't work. Trying what you're thinking won't work. I've been dealing with worse than you longer than you've been sucking air. I prefer you alive, but your corpse will do just fine. Try and pull on me, and it'll be the last thing you do."

Moss had underestimated him and had no doubt that he would make good on his promise. Moss felt hopeless and weak. He had no choice. "So, what now?"

"Now," Twelve said, coming close to pull Moss's weapon from his holster while keeping his own trained on Moss's head. "Now, you come with me."

Twelve jammed the second weapon in his pocket.

"You fucking people think you're so smart. You think everyone in the world is a fool," Twelve sneered, self-righteousness dripping from every word.

"You are a fool," Gibbs' voice echoed from behind the wall. Twelve turned.

"Wha—" he began as Moss cracked the man's arm against the wall and Gibbs jammed the barrel of his pistol in his mouth. His other hand reached to his pocket for Moss's weapon, but Moss was too quick, grabbing his arm before he had a chance to get it.

"Don't move," Gibbs snarled. "You've terrorized your last person today."

Twelve's eyes were wide with anger and fear. He thrashed hard and threw Moss back just long enough to reach for the weapon once more. He had misread Gibbs, whose eyes closed as he pulled the trigger of his pistol. The gun recoiled against Twelve's teeth, smoke, and the smell of burned flesh filling the small space.

The man's face cooked from within, blood seeped from orifices as the skin bubbled. His body slumped toward the floor as Moss held the man to keep blood from spilling onto the pristine floor.

Gibbs opened his eyes to see what he had done. His hand shook violently, and he cast his weapon clattering to the ground, bringing blood and gore with it.

"I did that," he sputtered. All the confidence from a moment before now drained from him.

"You did. You saved me," Moss whispered and grabbed a sleeping shirt to wrap around Twelve's face.

Gibbs stood like a statue.

"Gibbs, you saved me," Moss repeated, and his friend looked down at him. "But now you need to go. Go tell the others it's time and lead the march."

"Right," Gibbs said. He did not move.

Moss set the body down and stood, placing his hands on the sides of Gibbs' face. He looked into the eyes of his friend.

"You did great. You saved me from a world of torture and death. You stepped up and did what needed to be done. But now you have to do it again. For all of us," his words registered, and Gibbs blinked repeatedly.

"Right," and this time, he meant it. He turned and ran through the empty room, his footfalls echoing off the walls.

"Shit," Moss muttered. This was not how the plan was supposed to work. He had to act fast. He slid Twelve's wrist screen off his arm and replaced his own.

ERROR.

"Shit," Moss said again. The small internal computer was linked to the operator. He would need Judy to work on it if he had any hope of using it to access the VIP area. He dragged the body onto a cot, pulling a worn blanket over it. Moss knew this wouldn't work for long but hoped it would suffice long enough for him to set things in motion. He replaced his weapon with Twelve's, as it appeared to be a higher-end (and he hoped more functional) model.

As he exited down a long hallway out to the city, he heard Gibbs' voice resonating through the building. "They have taken advantage of us for too long. It's time we made our voices heard!" he hollered, followed by a cheer of rallied guards. Moss smiled, brimming with pride. His friend was doing it. He was leading, and people were following.

MOSS WAS SWEATING and panting when he reached the bar, and it didn't take his friends any time at all to read his face. They all stood as he entered, except Patchwork, who was still recovering. Moss tossed the wrist screen to Judy, who caught it easily.

"Need to make this work on me," he stated, and Judy flipped it over to examine the machine.

"On it," Judy said and got to work.

Ynna hustled over with Stan and Anders right behind. "The time is now," Moss said. "Bit of a change of plans. Stan, you're going to need to keep Patch safe while Ynna and Anders get the inmates riled. Judy will join you two when they finish with the armor. Gibbs is with the guards, so be careful once you get weapons."

"Right," Ynna said, nodding and flexing her mechanical hand. She and Anders rushed from the bar.

"You sure about this?" Stan asked, sounding disappointed that he would not be on the front lines.

"Yes," Moss told him. "There is no one better to keep him safe. Everything depends on Patch making contact with the outside and getting us access to weapons and vehicles. We are all counting on you keeping him safe."

"You'd do better if you had two arms," Judy snorted.

"Really? Now?" Stan bickered back.

"Yes, now!" Judy snarled. "We could use you at full strength."

"Being who I am makes me what I am, not some tech nonsense," Stan yelled.

Moss knew he needed to diffuse this before it became too distracting. "Get Patch to the tower and wait for me."

"Fine." Stan snorted and helped the young man to his feet.

"We got this," Patchwork forced from his mouth with a weak thumbs up.

"I know we do," Moss said as they hobbled toward the door.

"Stanley," Judy called after them, "I love you."

"I love you, too," Stan grumbled as he exited the door.

Judy was sitting at a table with a multi-tool which Moss had smuggled out of a supply closet. Pieces were already amassed before them, and Judy was flipping it over and over to look at the screen and the wiring on the back.

"How long?" Moss asked hurriedly. He kept checking the door to see if anyone was coming in but took some comfort in the fact that by now the guards would be marching on the wardens. Judy ignored his question and continued to work. Moss had always been enamored of Judy while they worked. No time was ever wasted, and there was a purpose to every movement which Moss found hypnotic.

Mr. Greene entered the bar, looking frazzled.

"So, it begins?" he asked loudly, not minding if the bartender heard him. They had used much of the money the guards had in the accounts to pay him handsomely for his silence.

"It does," Moss said, walking over and shaking the hand of his old mentor.

"What can I do?" he asked though he sounded to Moss as though he expected the answer.

"Stay safe," Moss pleaded. "Are you sure you don't want to join us? Get out of here?"

Moss had asked him almost daily and had always been met with the same answer. But this time, Mr. Greene seemed to be contemplating his words. He looked into Moss's eyes and pulled at his scraggly beard. "How bad is it going to get out there?" he finally asked.

"Pretty bad," Moss told him, "and all the worse for having known me."

Moss was not going to force the man to do anything, but he knew that if Mr. Greene stayed, he would likely not survive the days which followed. "Please," Moss said.

"Okay," Mr. Greene said, hanging his head in shame.

"I promise we will get your husband out," Moss assured him, knowing that was his major concern.

"I know you will," Mr. Greene said. His eyes were distant, as though lost in thought. "You know, before all this, we were working with a lab."

"That's wonderful," Moss exclaimed, truly happy for the man despite his guilt that his actions had prevented it.

"We had made all the arrangements and were just saving up our money," he explained, a slight smile crossed his lips at the thought.

Moss smiled, too. "You didn't want to adopt?"

"No, we wanted a kid who came from us. Designing her had been one of our greatest joys," he explained. His eyes had begun to mist over.

Moss closed the gap and embraced him. "You'll make great parents," Moss said, squeezing him. "She'll be lucky to have you."

"Thank you," Mr. Greene said and sobbed softly into Moss's shoulder.

After a moment, Judy announced, "Done."

Moss turned to get the device, but Mr. Greene held him for a moment. "You are an amazing man, Moss. Go do what you came here to do."

"I will," Moss said gratefully. He was amazed at the power of the words from his former boss. Twelve had possessed a leadership role but no leadership abilities. But here, stripped of everything, Mr. Greene could inspire. "Good luck."

Mr. Greene nodded and walked next to Moss over to the table at which Judy sat. They held up the device. "Should work now without an operator."

"Good work. Incredible," Moss remarked.

"Not really," Judy admitted, "Carcer tech hasn't really changed since I last worked with it."

"You see, sticking with outmoded technology is another sign of a poorly run business," Mr. Greene put in. He really did enjoy analyzing businesses. Even at this moment, he couldn't help but give his opinion.

Judy sighed, seeming utterly disinterested in his opinion. "Great story."

"He's coming with us, so play nice," Moss admonished.

Judy sighed again. "Fine. I'll keep him safe since I know you like him."

"Thank you?" Mr. Greene said dubiously.

"Thank you," Moss repeated. "Keep him by your side and be ready."

"I got you," Judy said and stood. "Do your thing."

Moss nodded, and they all headed out.

. . .

WORD WAS ALREADY BEGINNING to spread, and people were flooding to the streets. Prisoners rushed past Moss toward the center of the city. Even if they did not want to riot, people wanted to see what was going to happen.

One woman slowed to a brisk walk as she caught sight of Moss in his armor but broke back into a run as she moved beyond him. Shops were being closed or simply abandoned, and he moved in the opposite direction of the action, toward the VIP area. He shook his head, thinking about the moniker given to a place where the prisoners had even fewer freedoms than those in the city.

The tower loomed as Moss moved toward the edge of the city. It was constructed of red bricks set with metal hooks which curved downward toward the ground. A metal fence barred entry to the staircase. Stan guarded Patchwork who sat on the ground with his arms wrapped around his knees. Moss did not acknowledge them, waving instead to the guard looking out from the tower. He hardly seemed to notice, looking off in the distance at the assembling mob. Moss waved his hand over the locking mechanism at the gate, and it clicked, the door swinging loose.

As he moved through, he kicked a piece of loose brick between the door and the jamb so it could not magnetize fully closed. As he was under the lip of the tower, the guard above did not see the little nod Moss shot to Stan.

Moss ascended the steps in a hurry and spoke as he opened the lock to the tower office. "I'm here to relieve you."

The guard turned, looking tired and perplexed. He was an older man with thinning hair that formed a ring around a mostly bald head. Large bags hung heavy under keen eyes, and

Moss watched as the man's hand moved slightly toward an alert button.

"By you?" he asked dubiously.

Moss tried to act cool and shifted slightly, letting his hand fall on his weapon. "Yep."

"What's going on out there? The guests are all a-flurry but no one's answering comms," the guard said. His hand was moving closer to the alert as he spoke.

"Oh," Moss said, playing at casual. "You see—" And as he spoke, he drew Twelve's weapon and fired. In the instant Moss moved, the man looked unsurprised and reached for the button.

The bolt struck him too quickly, and he began convulsing. He reached in desperation, but his body failed him, and he flailed to the ground. Moss hurried over and took his weapon before binding his wrists behind his back with his own electronic cuffs.

Stan carried Patchwork to the vacated chair in front of a bank of three monitors. Moss handed Stan the guard's gun. "You keep him upright."

Stan snorted. "Do my best." Moss knew he was annoyed at his new assignment but didn't have the time to get into it.

"You gonna be alright?" Moss asked Patchwork as the young man set about his work on the computers.

Patchwork looked up, a crooked smile across his lips, "Well, I mean if you are giving me a choice?"

Moss smirked. It made him happy that even like this, with everything going on around them, the kid could still joke. "No, no, I am not," he said dryly.

Moss looked at Stan who nodded. "Go get Sandra. Burn would be proud," he said with a kind smile. Moss knew he was right and smiled as he exited.

He paused and stuck his head back through the door. "You know Judy is just looking out for you?"

"I know," Stan admitted with a wistful smile.

Moss thought about how he was able to disarm Twelve, and all that Stan had taught him. He wanted to inspire his friend. "And you know I couldn't have done any of this without what you've shown me?"

Stan's smile broadened. "I know. Go get her, man."

Moss tapped his hand against the doorjamb in acknowledgment and made his way to the bridge to the VIP area.

He passed through several gates to a long path flanked on both sides by chain-link squares containing the hovels of the highest value assets. The entire area stank of shit and Moss noticed plastic buckets of fecal matter set just inside the gates awaiting pickup.

"Some VIP area," he muttered, gripping his gun in anticipation of running into more guards. He saw none.

He had noticed the number ten spray-painted on the small shack in the video of his grandmother and was looking to see if he could find it in the labyrinth of cages. Infuriatingly, the numbers of the spaces did not appear to be in any sensical order, so Moss was left to hurry around like a headless chicken.

He knew that in the rest of the city, the guards were demanding benefits while the prisoners were preparing to riot, and time was not on his side. He ignored the pleas of prisoners who called out to him as he passed, wishing he could help but knowing that he could not. He tried to convince himself that they were in these cells for good reasons—that they were killers or rapists—but seeing them made him doubt it.

He scrambled down streets and alleyways, a sense of hopelessness and terror beginning to course through his veins. As he rounded one corner, what he saw struck him like a punch to the face.

CHAPTER 20

"Grimy?" Moss asked, the breath nearly sucked from his lungs.

The face his friend wore made Moss nervous—it was not that of elation but of worry. He recovered quickly and smiled, rushing over to give him an awkward embrace.

He was dressed in pristine blue linens with an armband similar to what the guards wore. The scrubs bore the Carcer logo on the breast pocket as well as an emblem indicating that he was a medical man.

"Moss, what are you doing here?" Grimy asked, looking up and down the street nervously.

Moss looked at him with puzzlement. "We are here to get you out. What are you doing here?"

He pulled on the Carcer emblem, and Grimy looked down, shifting uncomfortably. The energy he was putting off made Moss feel ill at ease. He knew it was a shock and that Grimy was always a bit aloof, but he seemed particularly peculiar.

"They pressed me into service," Grimy explained and cleared his throat.

"What do you mean?" Moss asked, forgetting momentarily about everything else he needed to be doing.

Grimy's posture changed. He shrunk down and held his arms close to his body. "When they learned that I was a makeshift medic, they asked if I wanted to do this rather than simply be a prisoner. I didn't think you would be coming for us so soon."

Moss shook his head in confusion. "But why help them? Why not just go into gen pop and meet up with the others?"

"I wanted to help," Grimy offered unconvincingly. Moss didn't know what to make of all this.

"Help?" he asked. "Help fucking Carcer?"

Grimy's demeanor turned icy. "I'm helping the prisoners, or guests, as it were. I'm helping the people in need here. It's my duty."

"You're a vet!" Moss exclaimed. "And a freedom fighter. Not some cooperate stooge."

At the mention of the word "vet," Grimy turned red with anger. He was a slight man and no fighter, but he looked to Moss as though he was getting ready to throw a punch. "Well, I'm sorry my wanting to help people doesn't align with your current philosophy."

Moss couldn't believe what he was hearing. He knew that Grimy was inclined to help but not like this, not helping people who wanted them dead. "Current philosophy? This has been our collective way of thinking," Moss nearly shouted. "Do you even want to get out of here?"

Moss asked, and the look on Grimy's face sent a chill down his spine. It was calculating and in a way which Moss had never seen, and it made him nervous. His heart broke at what he was thinking.

"Oh," Grimy muttered, shuffling his feet, "yes, of course, I want to leave."

Moss looked into the man's eyes. "Grimy, what did they ask you about when they took you in?"

"Pardon?" Grimy looked genuinely confused.

"What did they ask you about when they took you in?" Moss repeated slowly, the words heavy as they left his mouth.

"Oh, nothing much. They wanted to know our evil plans and how we had pulled off the ThutoCo job, that sort of thing," he explained, but the words were shaky.

Moss let his head drop a moment, staring at the filthy ground beneath his feet before asking, "And did they ask you about me?"

He looked up to see Grimy shake his head vigorously. "No, not really."

"Oh, Grimy," Moss exhaled. He felt as though all his strength had been sapped from him. "You've never been a very good liar."

"Pardon?" Grimy said defensively, but Moss could see through it. Grimy seemed to know the jig was up. He dropped his head and began to weep. Moss put one hand on Grimy's shoulder and the other on Twelve's pistol.

"How did they get you?" Moss asked, his heart breaking.

"Please," Grimy whimpered.

"I'm not going to do anything. I just need to know," Moss assured him. He didn't know what to do. He was enraged at the betrayal but sad for his friend.

"They," Grimy began, wiping tears and mucus from his face. "They picked me up outside the perfumery a month ago. They had me, threatened me. I didn't want to be tortured, abused. I couldn't take it. I cracked. But I only told them a little. Just enough so they would let me go. Please, Moss, you have to believe me."

Moss's hand was vibrating with rage. He looked at the sad husk of the man who had once saved the life of his best friend, the man who had taken in Ynna when she was beaten nearly to death. Betrayal, rage, and misery coursed through him, leaving him unable to think. He felt his thumb click the gun to lethal.

"You didn't want to be hurt. Because of you, everyone was hurt. Stan was beaten, and Patch still hasn't recovered. CT is fucking dead. Thrown from a roof because you didn't want to pay the price that comes with this life? I've had to murder people to get here. Gibbs had to betray everything he believes to get you out. We've all paid, and," Moss said as he pulled the weapon from its holster. "And CT is fucking dead!" he repeated.

Grimy fell to his knees, sobbing and holding his hands up. "I didn't want any of that! I never wanted to hurt you!"

"You knew what would happen to us. To all of us. I'm just lucky I snuck out, right?" Moss accused.

Grimy nodded, tears streaming to the ground beneath him. "I'm sorry."

"Of course, you're sorry. Everyone is fucking sorry when they get caught," Moss said with disgust. "So, what? You betray us, and you get to live out your days as a Carcer medic? That about it?"

Grimy said nothing. He continued to sniffle and cry.

Moss pulled out the gun. Grimy let out a wail.

"Please, Moss," Grimy said. Looking at the pathetic shell of the man, Moss's heart broke once more.

"You know the price," Moss said, his own voice shaking, eyes burning. He did not want to do what he knew he had to. Burn had always made the cost of betrayal clear to all of them.

"I didn't," Grimy stuttered.

"I have to know," Moss began. "What did you tell them. Actually. What do they know?"

The words choked from his mouth, "Not much, I swear it."

"Tell me!" Moss thundered, pointing the weapon.

Grimy raised his hands defensively. "They know," was all he could force.

"Know what?" he asked through gritted teeth. A cold sweat broke out on his forehead. His hand trembled.

"They know you have the program, that your father made you a weapon against the AIC," he admitted, sounding as though a burden was lifted from him.

"Fuck, Grimy," Moss said, letting the gun in his hand fall slack for a moment.

Grimy didn't try to reach for the weapon or stop what he knew was coming, he simply looked up at Moss with a tear-stained face. "My name is Terrence. You know I hate that nickname. Burn thought that he was so clever."

At the mention of Burn's name, Moss tightened his grip on the weapon, pressing his finger hard against the trigger guard. "That so? Well, maybe you could have said something rather than selling us all down the river?"

"I didn't mean for any of this to happen," Grimy pleaded.

Moss scoffed with disgust. "Oh, yeah, Grimy. What the fuck did you think would happen?"

"I'm—I'm sorry, Moss," he said again.

Moss was miserable. He hated how he felt. Hated what the man had done, what it had caused, and the void left by misplaced trust. His body vibrated with the intensity of it all.

Grimy looked right into his eyes. "So, what now? You're going to kill me, I suppose?"

"Grimy or Terrence, whatever the fuck, you destroyed everything we worked for. Got us killed and imprisoned. Gave our enemies everything they needed," Moss seethed. He moved forward, pressing the gun against Grimy's forehead, causing him to burst into tears again. "But you seem to have forgotten one thing."

Grimy looked up at him with misery in his eyes. He forced, "What's that?"

"We're the good guys," Moss said and raised the gun,

bringing the butt crashing down on his old friend's head. Grimy fell to the ground with a light thud. A small trickle of blood escaped a minor gash. He would wake in pain but would survive. Moss knew what Burn would have done, what many of the others would have done, but he couldn't kill Grimy. He had sold them out, betrayed them to the enemy, but he had helped them, too. He had done so much for them, and Moss couldn't execute him the way their enemies would have no qualm in doing. They were better than that.

He also knew that Grimy would have already given Carcer everything he had. He would be no help to them anymore. He had made his bed, and now he would sleep in it.

MISERABLY, Moss turned to look around and try to get his bearings. He still had a job to do, and running into Grimy had chewed into time he didn't have. As he looked, he caught sight of a prisoner who had been watching the whole thing unfold. She simply stared at Moss with hollow eyes, reflecting how he felt. Neither said a word.

Moss shrugged, not knowing what else to do and began walking again as if in a haze. He tried to shake the feeling and get back to his mission, but he was distracted.

Hey guys, Moss heard Seti's familiar Australian accent in his mind's ear, communicated through the neural implant in his head. It felt as if it had been so long since he had used this. But for the first time in what felt like a long time, his lip twitched into a smile. Patchwork had gotten through to the outside.

Seti, it's great to hear from you, Ynna said.

Oh, you're all in C City, Seti said, clearly having got a read on their location. *What can I do?*

Start looking for some safe routes out of here and be ready to let us know, Ynna ordered.

On it, Seti replied.

Gibbs chimed in, *Things are getting pretty hairy over here.*

Yeah, no shit. Out here, too, Ynna added. *Moss, you find your grandmother?*

No, not yet, Moss thought to them.

Things are about to get pretty real pretty quick, so perhaps you could hurry along? Ynna suggested.

Moss hadn't planned on telling them about Grimy until he saw them but needed them to know he wasn't simply wasting time. *I found Grimy*, he informed them.

That's great, Gibbs put in.

I don't see him on comms, Seti pointed out.

Moss sighed. *He was working with Carcer*, he told them finally. *I'll fill you all in later, but he won't be joining us.*

No, he heard Ynna say. Even through the transmission, he could hear the pain in her. He imagined her stopping amidst the throng of rioting prisoners, realizing the reality of it. His heart broke for her as it had for himself.

I'm sure you guys have heaps of emotions now, but it seems like you have things you need to do, Seti offered by way of distraction. *Moss, I've got a fix on your location. Where are you trying to get?*

Cage ten, Moss said. He waited in silence. He wanted to say something more to Ynna but could not think of the words.

Time passed excruciatingly.

Seti spoke after what felt like an age. *Two rights and a left.*

Thank you, Moss said, truly grateful.

He hurried down the narrow alleyways, ignoring the shouts from the prisoners.

He saw the spray-painted ten and stopped. The old woman from the video, the grandmother he had not seen for years, knelt over a small flower growing in a tin can.

Panting, elated, and overwhelmed, Moss did not know what to say. He said the only thing he could think. "Grandma?"

The woman's shoulders raised defensively, and she turned one cautious eye to face him. When she saw his face, she gasped.

"M—Moss?"

CHAPTER 21

S he got to her feet as quickly as her frail and beaten body
would allow. She looked at him with a disbelief he didn't
think possible.

"I'm guessing you don't work for Carcer?" she asked with an
absolute smile, joy replacing the shock.

Moss grinned, his heart racing. "No. No, I do not."

He waved his wrist over the lock, and it beeped before
clicking open. He pulled on the gate to hug his grandmother. It
did not budge.

"Oh, honey, it gets stuck," Sandra chuckled. "You have to lift
and pull."

He did as instructed and swung the door open. He grabbed
her and pulled her in tight, her slight frame thumping against
the armor. He wept into her white hair.

"I cannot believe you came for me," she said. Though overcome with emotion, she did not shed a tear.

Moss pulled himself together, releasing her and saying, "I
came as soon as I could."

She cocked her head at him. "Brave and stupid, just like me."

"Certainly seems that way," he said. Going from seeing Grimy to seeing her left his head spinning.

"We leaving now?" she asked, her demeanor shifting. In an instant, she had become all business, her eyes shifting and mind strategizing.

"We are," Moss said, wondering how things were going for the rest of the crew.

"Bring me a weapon?" she asked. He had not considered that she would want one and felt foolish at his own surprise at the question.

She had been a leader her whole life. First in the military and then with Burn. He fished in his pocket for his gun.

"Give me the shit one, eh?" she joked, nodding toward Twelve's weapon holstered at Moss's side.

He smirked. "I earned this one."

"I'll bet you did," she said with an approving smile.

It was odd to Moss that they were engaging this way. He knew they could catch up after they were free from the city, but he had so many questions, so much he wanted to discuss with her.

They made their way back toward the tower. He had been so lost—he hadn't realized how sprawling this area was, and it would take time to get back.

"They told me they killed Burn?" she stated as a question. Her once strong body was not able to keep a good pace with Moss.

He slowed. "They did."

Sandra snorted. "Bastard go down fighting?"

Through the hardness, there was an unmistakable misery in her question.

"What do you think?" Moss asked in an attempt to buoy her spirits.

"Heard through the grapevine that you gave it to them good," she said, not wanting to dwell on her dead lover.

"We did. Dad's program worked," Moss explained. They were getting closer to the tower, and Moss wanted to check in with the others but couldn't divide his attention. "Lost the program in the explosion, though."

She looked on him then with an expression that told him she knew something more than he did. "Oh," she said.

"What?" Moss asked. He was tired of feeling as if he was always playing catch-up with anything relating to his family.

"We have a lot to discuss, but now ain't the time," she told him, raising her weapon and firing before Moss even saw the guard. Her aim had been precise, and the bolt hit the guard in the neck before he even knew it was fired.

"Whoa," Moss uttered.

"You'll get there," she assured him with a pat on the back.

"What don't I know?" Moss asked, not yet willing to let the issue drop.

Sandra gave a slight shrug. "Listen, kid, your dad was a good and noble man, but he was short-sighted. Your mom and I made some alterations, so there is more to that program than you know."

For the second time since seeing her, he was surprised when he felt he shouldn't be. It only left him with more questions. He was not able to ask as they heard gunshots emanating from the direction of the tower.

"Go ahead, I'll catch up," Sandra commanded. Moss didn't question the order and ran toward the sound, pulling his weapon free.

Status report? Moss commanded, but as he thought it, he heard more gunfire popping off around the city. He couldn't tell if it had just begun or if he hadn't noticed because he was too focused on his grandmother.

Got weapons and we are moving on the depot, Judy said.

Gibbs came through just as Judy finished. *We were mid-walk-out, but the guards are mobilizing now.*

How you looking, Moss? Ynna asked.

Got her, heading to the tower now, Moss thought.

Get here quick Moss. Stan is up against it, Patchwork said.

His robotic legs carried Moss quickly toward the tower, and he saw two guards with their backs to him taking shots at the tower. More were making their way up the stairs with One behind, her weapon drawn and ready for action.

Two shots made short work of the guards and Moss hopped over them with ease, moving toward the tower. The guards on the stairs noticed the commotion and turned toward Moss, spraying the area with bullets and bolts. He leaped between two cages as the world around him erupted into sparks, explosions, and hissing metal. Dirt and smoke filled his lungs as he tried to get his bearings, crawling back around so he could peek out when the guards reloaded.

But One was no fool. She had brought well-trained men with her who would pop off shots with enough frequency to keep him suppressed. He crawled around to try and flank them. He worried for a moment that his grandmother would come down the street and be picked off, but he knew she was smarter than that. He crawled left around one of the cages.

The prisoner housed by where Moss was crawling stuck her head out of the shack, attracting the attention of the guards. They fired warning shots into the tin structure, and she retreated quickly. Moss moved around the cage, using the shack as cover. As he crept around, he saw Stan standing in the door with his weapon drawn. Moss made a bird call the way Stan had shown him, and the chain-link erupted over his head. Working hard to keep his eyes open amidst the gunfire, Moss watched as

Stan bound through the door, using his one arm to fire down the stairs. One of the guards fell backward, knocking into the other. The second guard was hit from a shot which came from the street. He slumped, too, and the area was silent.

Stan looked down the street. "Sandra!" he called out, a massive smile on his face.

"Stanley," she called back, but Moss was already up and running.

"Stan!" he called out as One leaped up from the railing behind him, the weapon raised in an instant. Stan turned as she, Sandra and Moss all fired their weapons at once.

One was rocketed back against the railing as Stan's chest burst open with blood. The linen shirt did nothing to protect him from the bullet. His eyes went wide as he fell to his knees, clutching at the wound. Dark crimson seeped through his fingers, and he coughed, blood pouring from his mouth.

"Stanley," Sandra cried again as she rushed over to him.

Moss was at his side in a moment as well, and Patchwork emerged from the office. Patch looked down at the blood through swollen eyes and vomited.

"Good to see you, Sandra," Stan sputtered.

They knelt by his side.

"You've come so far. I'm proud of what you've done, young man," Sandra soothed. It was obvious that she had comforted the dying before as she took his hand in hers. Misery coated her face.

"Thanks, coach," Stan murmured, his eyes rolling around, unable to focus. "Moss?"

"I'm right here, Stan," Moss said, unable to contain his emotions.

"You keep it up, make this worth it," Stan asked, blinking rapidly, his shirt soaked through.

Moss felt his face contort as he promised, "I will."

"And tell," Stan said, his mouth so coated in blood, he was nearly unable to speak. "Tell Judy I love them. Make sure they're okay. They'll need you now."

"I will," Moss promised through the tears.

"We both will," Sandra added.

Stan smiled at them. "Thanks, guys." His breathing was becoming shallow. "Promise you'll think of me when you get that pizza," he said with a wide, crazed grin.

Moss put a hand on the massive man's neck and pressed their heads together. "Every time."

The breaths came slower until they ceased.

"Stan!" Moss wailed, and Patchwork collapsed, gripping the railing for support.

"Cocksucker!" Sandra shouted, turning her attention to One.

The warden was pressed against the railing beyond Patchwork, breathing heavily. She was wounded, but her antiquated armor had done well to dampen the shots. Sandra stalked over to the woman and gripped her armor at the neck.

"Corporate scum," Sandra hissed in the woman's face.

"Please," One forced. "I don't want to die."

The woman had been so tough when Moss had met her, and now she seemed pathetic and weak.

"Oh, you'll die. You'll all fucking die for what you do to the citizens of this world," she snarled. She punched One hard in the nose. Her body may have been weakened from years of confinement, but she was no less tough.

She struck the woman again and again, cracking her nose and popping her eyes. Blood cascaded around, and it struck Moss that, in that moment, his grandmother reminded him of Stan.

One was thoroughly dead when Sandra finally stood.

"We can't tell Judy, not yet," Sandra panted, blood dripping from her hand. Her eyes were hard and determined.

"They'll know when we get there," Moss reminded her.

"We will deal with it then," Sandra said and shook the blood from her fist. Seeing her at that moment, Moss thought about when bikers had jumped him upon arriving in BA City. He had been a different person then, a skinny, scared kid. But with his back against the wall, he had shot a biker instinctively. He had never understood where the strength to do that had come from, but seeing his grandmother now, he understood he had some of her buried deep within him.

Moss looked at Patchwork, who was clearly in shock. The kid had sliced through a Carcer guard with a sword before, but it was obvious that watching his friend die had shaken him terribly. Moss walked over and put his hands on the young man's shoulders.

"You gonna be alright?" he asked.

"I don't know, man. Maybe?" he stuttered.

"Holy shit, you Jo's boy? You're a spitting image," Sandra said.

"Y—Yes, ma'am, I am," he said, looking at her with a hint of recognition.

Sandra snorted. "I'm Sandra, if you didn't remember. Bit shocked your old mom let you run with this lot."

Patchwork flashed a weak smile. "She's not thrilled about it."

Sandra chuckled. "I'm sure she ain't."

"You good to go?" Moss asked, though he wasn't sure of the answer to that himself. With everything that had happened in the last few minutes and Stan's body not yet cold at his feet, he almost didn't have the will to go on. He could not even imagine how Judy would react.

At that moment, he wished he had killed Grimy.

"I still have to get the doors open," Patchwork said, returning

Moss to the here and now. "Just the main gates I mean, not the depots."

"Right," Moss said, "can you do it remotely?"

"It'll take longer, but you know I can do it," Patch said with his usual confidence.

"Then let's ride," Sandra said, and they all turned to run toward the vast prison city and the sounds of gunfire and chaos.

CHAPTER 22

Smoke filled their lungs as Moss, Patchwork, and Sandra ran toward the center of the city. The prisoners had set fire to structures and ash and embers pirouetted through the air. People screamed as guards tried to push their way around in full riot gear. Others threw rocks and shot at the drones which buzzed overhead, sending them fluttering around like possessed hummingbirds.

"We have to get through them," Sandra said, pointing to a mass of bodies which blocked the street toward the depot.

A young man near the back was screaming obscenities and holding an old revolver over his head. Many of the prisoners were now armed though few seemed interested in using them on the guards with their superior firepower. Moss snatched the pistol from the young man who turned and looked on him with rage.

Moss was thankful he had the foresight to bring clothes to wear over his armor so that he could blend in with the crowd, but the man was about to speak when Moss fired into the air. The sound sent people cowering, and they were able to push through toward the depot.

Three guards were blocking the narrow space between the buildings forming a shield wall with Gibbs at their back. Moss smiled; his friend was exactly where he needed to be. He had been worried that in the confusion, it might have been difficult, but he had done it.

Now, Gibbs, Moss told him, and he watched as Gibbs loosened his weapon and fired into the backs of the guards one after the other. They were too confused to react, and they fell in quick succession, only stunned, but down.

At seeing a guard help in their plight, the crowd erupted into a cheer and surged forward. Moss, Patch, and Sandra were pushed forward in the direction of the buildings which contained their rides to freedom.

The parking plaza was already filled with prisoners who had broken through from other directions. They were pushing over vans and trucks, climbing on top and cheering wildly. Gibbs was being patted on the back by prisoners as he pulled a loose shirt over his armor. In the mayhem, they didn't want him to be confused for a proper guard and be killed.

"You did it," Moss said to him. "Great work."

Gibbs beamed. "Bought us just enough time. We were nearly coming to blows when the word came that the guests were rioting."

"I'm so proud of you," Moss said, and he truly was.

Gibbs smiled with pride but nodded to the chaos around them and said, "We've still got a ways to go."

"Patch, how's it coming?" Moss asked the young man, one of his enhanced eyes black with work.

"Doing my best," Patchwork said, slightly defensively. "Working on getting open depot six. It was the biggest one, and I figure it's got the best ride."

"Good thinking," Moss told him, looking around for the largest building in the area.

Spotting it, he thought, *Let's meet at depot six.*

Copy, Ynna transmitted. They heard a gunshot from down a street which Moss took to be Ynna indicating their location.

They pushed through the rioters and formed a ring around Patchwork who knelt next to the massive metal door, his second eye going black.

"The wardens are getting geared up with digital plate armor and will probably be on us soon," Gibbs told them. "It's going to get worse before it gets better."

"It always does," Moss observed, his weapon aimed up one street. Several streets converged on this location, but Moss figured they would be coming from the direction of the barracks.

"Burn taught you well," Sandra noted with a smile.

"They all have," Moss said, feeling the need to pay homage to Stan and the others.

His grandmother nodded.

Many prisoners began rushing down the street, away from the barracks, fleeing in terror and hollering for help.

"Let them come," Gibbs said, grim determination in his voice.

Hurry, Moss told the others.

Nearly to you, Ynna said.

It was taking longer to get from weapon storage to the depot than they had calculated, and Moss was worried they were about to be surrounded and killed before they could make their escape.

The place fell silent as the fleeing prisoners cowered behind those few with weapons or the parked vehicles. All eyes were pointed down the street, awaiting the wardens.

The silence persisted a moment longer before several metallic plunks echoed through the air. Gas canisters flew from the street down into the assembled masses. Moss and Gibbs fumbled to get their masks out from under the linen pants they wore to conceal their armor. Sandra ripped the sleeves from her shirt, wrapping one over Patchwork's nose and mouth before doing her own. Her natural eyes would be stinging before too long, and Moss tried to offer her his mask.

She shook her head. "Ain't my first time."

Moss nodded and pulled the mask over his face, knowing that she would be able to handle the gas better than he.

The drones which had scattered returned, raining rubber shots into the crowd, the screams beginning anew. Moss knew the wardens well enough to know that they would show them no such kindness as to use non-lethal ammunition. The three fired into the sky, knocking out some of the drones.

Moss watched as two augmented prisoners braved the gas and began working on the drones, presumably to turn them into weapons against the wardens.

Lights pierced the clouds as the wardens appeared from the street. Fully encased in electronic armor, the metal-plated people appeared more as drudges than humans. Tall, and moving with robotic efficiency, they strode into the open space.

"Cease and desist!" one of the wardens demanded through a loudspeaker set into the shoulder of the machine.

Moss knew they didn't have time and fired a burst of shots toward the wardens. He had aimed for the joints, and some of the shots found paydirt, causing one of the arms of the leader to swing out wildly. He listened as the arm-mounted machine guns of the wardens began to spin to life.

"Got it," Patchwork said, and the ground shook as the massive doors behind them began to open.

The space around them erupted as the wardens began to fire in their direction, shredding the vehicles between them.

As soon as there was enough space to squeeze through, they

ducked into the garage, Moss, and Sandra firing back in the direction of the wardens.

"The shoulder again!" Gibbs cried out as he clutched a bullet hole.

The doors ground to a stop. "I'm holding the program until we can get out of here," Patch told them. His eyes went black again, and several drones turned their fire on the wardens. The rubber bullets did nothing but confuse them and force them to take their aim skyward. The Carcer officers shot their own drones out of the air, sending heaps of metal careening to the ground.

From behind a van, the two prisoners peeked out with their rewired drones and fired more shots at the wardens. More confusion ensued as they had to divide their fire. Mr. Greene had been right that wardens would not work as a unified force, and they all seemed to be firing in different directions with no solid plan of attack.

A rocket whistled through the air, blasting two of the wardens into pieces. The prisoners roared with delight as Judy reloaded, rushing toward the depot with Anders, Ynna and Mr. Greene at their back. They peppered the wardens with machine gun fire as they moved between the parked vehicles, sliding along the sides for cover.

"Oh," Gibbs said, and Moss turned to look at his friend who was gazing into the garage with astonishment. Moss followed his eyes, the beam of light from the cracked door illuminating a huge military-style dropship.

"Wow," Patchwork said, seeming to notice it for the first time as well.

Gibbs smiled through the pain. "That'll do, pig."

Moss turned back to see Judy fire another rocket, which missed the wardens and blasted against a building, sending dust and debris into the dissipating gas. The ground tremored as the building collapsed and knocked the weakened Patchwork to the ground. Judy was out of shots and into the garage, covered in dust, with the others right behind.

Ynna seemed to register their numbers before Judy. "Fuck," she shouted as Patchwork began closing the doors.

They stopped after only a meter.

"Counter hackers," Patchwork said, "I'll focus on opening the roof."

Judy looked around. "No."

Sandra gripped Judy by the shoulders. "Stanley went out a hero, and we need you right now."

"No!" Judy wailed again, pushing and thrashing against the old woman who pulled them in tight, whispering something Moss could not hear.

He had met a lot of tough people since leaving the Burb and counted Judy among the toughest, but now they cried soft tears into Sandra's shoulder. Moss had to look away, unable to watch the misery.

Anders ran into the ship, his boots clanging up the gangway.

Moss looked around. "Where's Mr. Greene?" he asked frantically.

Ynna, looking exhausted with a bullet wound in her thigh, said, "I thought he was right behind us."

Moss dropped Twelve's pistol and snatched the rifle from her hands and started to squeeze through the giant door.

"I'll come," Gibbs offered, but Moss waved him off.

"No, get Patch onboard and be ready for us," Moss ordered, "Ynna, watch my back."

She slung another rifle from her back and nodded as Moss ran out into the gray haze. He couldn't see much and moved in the direction from which they had come. He was accustomed to the constant fog which sat heavy on BA City, but this was entirely different. His mask hissed as he breathed heavily, trying to find his way.

Vague shapes of trucks were everywhere, and he passed prisoners huddling for safety, thick layers of dust covering their forms. Beams of light cut through as the wardens moved in his direction. One turned slightly and saw him, Moss popping off shots at the head. Glass and metal cracked and dinged until he saw red from the inside of the metal casing and the machine ground to a halt.

He heard his heartbeat through the ringing in his ears after all the explosions and nearby gunfire. The ground shook once more as the topside garage door began to open. Moss was grateful for the skill of young Patchwork.

He heard a cough and rushed in that direction, seeing Mr. Greene in the ground with his back against a truck. Coated in ash and debris, he looked like some surreal living statue. He was holding on to his side as Moss knelt beside him.

"Got shot," Mr. Greene said.

Moss moved his hands to reveal the wound. It was only a slight graze of his ribs but bleeding enough to terrify a man who had spent his life behind a desk.

"You'll be all right," Moss assured him, putting an arm around his waist and hoisting him up. He winced as Moss brought him to his feet.

"Thank you for coming back," Mr. Greene wheezed.

Moss smiled. "Of course."

They moved back toward the ship, the lights from the wardens shifting around, looking for them. They were closing in on them, and Moss knew he had little time to get Mr. Greene to safety.

His robotic legs carried him quickly, but his old mentor couldn't keep up, his steps dragging as he moved. He saw the shape in the doorway, Ynna waving them on, but the door was opening. Patchwork couldn't keep Carcer from taking control back. He breathed slightly easier since he could still hear the rooftop door opening.

Moss saw the shape of his head silhouetted in the dust as a warden's light found him. He sent them both crashing to the ground as bullets cut overhead. The dust swirled and danced as Moss heard Ynna return fire. The warden crashed down just behind them, and he heaved Mr. Greene up and moved him to the door. Six more lights were following him toward the depot as Ynna rushed and helped carry Mr. Greene to the ramp of the ship.

It was already hovering off the ground, ready to move skyward as Ynna was shot from behind. It glanced off her hip and caused her to fall, bringing the other two with her. Gibbs rushed to help her onboard as Moss helped Mr. Greene to his feet once more. They were so close to the ship, but the wardens began laying down fire blind.

Two of the guns mounted on the side of the ship returned fire, causing the lights to shift as the wardens moved for cover.

Gibbs returned as the ship began to lift toward the open roof, the direct sunlight blinding. Gibbs helped to pull Mr. Greene aboard as the gunfire renewed from both directions.

Moss's vision went white with pain as he felt several bullets pierce his body. As if in slow motion, he felt his body fall to the earth as Mr. Greene's foot disappeared into the ship. With a grunt, he lifted himself up and put a hand on the ascending ramp. As the side of the ship vibrated and tore, Moss felt a hand on his wrist.

Gibbs looked over, terrified as the ship continued to rise. He felt his feet lift from the ground.

"I got you!" Gibbs screamed, trying to get a good grip on Moss's arm. Moss threw his other hand onto the ramp, trying to get a grip. He began to lift himself as he felt it.

A bullet passed right through his forearm. He lost his grip and slid. Gibbs held his other hand as the ship lifted.

"Hold on!" Gibbs cried, holding on to Moss with one hand and the ship with the other. Moss lifted his arm, but he could not use his fingers. He felt another shot pass through him, and he lost his grip, his hand sliding into Gibbs's.

The ship continued to lift slowly as Moss felt the fabric of his glove begin to rip.

"Stop the ship!" Gibbs shouted into the ship, but Moss knew he wasn't heard. The fabric ripped a little more. "It can't happen like this!"

"Fly, you idiot," Moss said as Gibbs looked back at him, tears streaking through the dirt on his face.

"That's not the line," Gibbs wailed in misery and confusion.

The fabric tore again.

Moss had gotten what he came for. He had saved his grandmother and freed his friends. He was proud of what he had done. If the fall didn't kill him, the wardens certainly would. He made his peace with it. He had accomplished a lot and had set his friends up for future success.

The last piece ripped, and he felt his body begin to fall to the ground.

Gibbs shouted something, one loose glove in his hand.

Moss's legs telescoped and took most of the impact as he hit the ground, watching as the ship blotted out the sun. He knew Gibbs was going to try and turn the ship around but also knew Anders was too smart for that. What looked like hundreds of lines of machine gun fire followed the ship as it moved. It shifted wildly to avoid a rocket launched from the ground before disappearing behind the lip of the roof.

Moss smiled.

He knew that Burn would be proud that he got Sandra out. He knew that Mr. Greene's husband would be elated to see him freed. His heart broke for Judy and Gibbs. Above all, he hoped his friends wouldn't be foolish enough to try to come for him.

He sputtered blood as the imposing figures of the wardens surrounded him.

The head of one of the chassis hissed open, blowing smoke and dirt in a plume, and he saw the unmistakable face of Warden Ninety-Nine revealed from within.

Moss laughed. Of all the wardens, here was this asshole was again.

He smirked under his mustache. "I knew you'd come," he snarled with pride.

"Of course, I did," Moss said in nearly a whisper, "we are the good guys."

THE END

EPILOGUE

"Stanley Wu was killed in a riot in Carcer City One earlier this week when the guests became violent against the hardworking employees. This marks a sad day for BA City Miners fans who remember Wu's game clinching goal against Jerusalem in the ND Cup four years ago. After being injured on the pitch, sources tell us that Wu became troubled and fell in with undesirable characters, even being linked to the terrorist attack on ThutoCo this year," said the blonde broadcaster whose hologram was being projected into the room. She raised a hand, indicating for the viewer to look to her left as Ndeke Miller, the Miner's current star striker appeared next to her.

"It's sad," he said, eyes downcast before looking into the camera. "It really goes to show what happens when you turn your back on your fans, sponsors and teammates."

He continued to speak as the door to the conference room opened and Arthur Smith, President of ThutoCo, entered. He was angry and Alice Carcer did not stand for him when he stepped in.

He turned to see the broadcast.

"You see how Derek is covering this?" Alice asked absently.

"He has D2E running these stories all day. No one is better at controlling the narrative."

"No one believes the news anyway," Arthur said, folding his arms across his chest.

Alice simply smiled. "You're a fool if you believe he doesn't control the forums too. That short pants wearing dolt has the public wrapped around his finger."

Arthur felt his blood boil as she suggested he didn't understand how the world worked. "That's not what I'm here to talk about, Alice. You have something that belongs to me."

She steepled her long fingers. "Your employee was caught inciting a riot in a Carcer facility. He will be returned to you once he has been processed."

Arthur knew he needed to tread carefully. Since Moss had helped destroy much of ThutoCo's technology, Arthur had discovered that the young man had immensely valuable programs uploaded to his neural chip. He needed the kid and the information he possessed.

Arthur knew another thing: he couldn't let Alice know how valuable an asset she had. She would try to tap his chip, use her breakers to extract the intel. If those breakers made a mistake though, a self-destruct sequence would initiate, and everything would be lost.

"We had a significant bounty on him long before you captured him and your own bylaws state that the initial bounty holder has rights to the arrested," Arthur told her. His lawyers had spent countless sleepless nights coming up with an ironclad argument he could use on her.

Though the Amalgamated Interests Council was Arthur's brainchild and theoretically supposed to be working toward one common goal, the heads of the planet's major companies were often at odds. They shook hands and played nice while they employed teams to undermine and sabotage one another.

Alice stared at him, her ever unblinking blue eyes piercing him. "Don't speak to me of bylaws, I write the bylaws." She smiled knowingly. "What your lawyers may not have told you is that the arrested belong to the highest bidder."

She brought up a bounty on the screen, with a value and time stamp. "As you can see, we outbid you just before we took your employee into custody. He is ours."

Arthur nearly spit as he read the screen. He was outbid by almost nothing, a mere one thousand more than ThutoCo had bid. Even more egregious was the time stamp. The Carcer bounty had been posted a minute before the supposed time of arrest.

He had been outwitted, outplayed by the person who had taken his position on the council.

He hated Alice. He wanted to reach across the desk and throttle her. He wanted to wring the necks of his lawyers for not catching this.

He vowed to make her, and everyone else who stood in his way pay.

"As I said, though, I will do you a courtesy," Alice smiled. "Once we have what we need, we will return him to you."

"Unbroken," Arthur demanded.

"You are in no position to order me around," she shifted her body slightly and the ceremonial saber at her side rattled against her chair. "But I assure you we have our best people on it."

Arthur held back a smile. She had said too much. If she had her, "best people on it," she had no doubt transferred Moss to The Table, Carcer's main base of international operations.

He smiled as sweetly as he could muster. "Thank you for that."

He saw Alice's eye twitch and he wondered if she had figured out his plan. She would no doubt have elite guards watching the facility, but Arthur was confident that his BurbSec Zetas could break in and extract Moss without Carcer being any the wiser.

Alice would have her suspicions but would never be able to prove it.

His team was trained by disgruntled former Carcer operatives and knew all the secrets Alice tried to hide. He would get what was his.

He had his plan, but he still wanted to shame Alice before the meeting was through.

"I hear you traded one valuable asset for another," he stated, cocking his head with superiority.

Alice scoffed. "That old woman is worth nothing. While she was housed in Carcer City, we beat every last piece of information out of her."

Arthur let out a laugh. "If you believe that, I've got some property on Mars to sell you. That, "old woman," is one of the greatest warriors BA City has ever seen and her skills turned the tide against Andreas during the war. As long as she breathes, she's a threat. And now, she hates Carcer more than ever. I'd watch my back if I were you."

"I have an army to watch my back," Alice seethed, her normal calm demeanor temporarily cracked. "Who watches yours?"

"The entire AIC watches mine," Arthur gloated. "You may have a new position, but I am the one who is striking deals with the off-worlders. I am the one who is ensuring the future we are all striving towards."

Alice grinned and stood. "You continue to tell yourself that."

As her hologram began to fade, she said, "I'll say hello to Moss for you."

NOTE TO THE READER

Thanks for reading *Corroded Cells: A Cyberpunk Saga (Book 2)*. If you enjoyed the book, please leave a review; it is incredibly helpful to new authors. Reviews are one of the ways in which people can discover new work and help me to create more of it. Thanks again for reading.

For more information and bonus content, visit Thutoworld.com

AUTHOR BIO

Matthew A. Goodwin has been writing about spaceships, drag-
ons, and adventures since he was twelve years old. His passion
for fantasy began when he discovered a box set of the Hobbit
radio drama on cassette tape in his school's library at the age of
seven. He fell in love with fantasy worlds and soon discovered
D&D and Warhammer miniatures.

Not wanting to be limited by worlds designed by others, he
created Thutopia (now called the Thuton Empire), a fantasy
world of his own, which he still writes about to this day.

Like many kids with an affinity for fantasy, a love of science
fiction soon followed. He loved sweeping space operas and gritty
cyberpunk stories which asked questions about man's relationship to technology. That led him to write his first published
work, *Into Neon: A Cyberpunk Saga*, which takes place in a larger
science fiction universe.

He has a passion for travel and wildlife, and when he is not
off trying to see the world, he lives in San Francisco with his wife
and son.

Made in the USA
Las Vegas, NV
22 March 2021